# Snowfall on the City
## Science Fiction Tales

## Jennifer Rachel Baumer

## Monstrosity Ink

### Reno, Nevada

Snowfall on the City
Science Fiction Tales

ISBN – 13: 978-0692244319 (Monstrosity Ink)
ISBN – 10: 069224431X

"*Snowfall on the City*" © 2010
Originally appeared in Aoife's Kiss #34, September 2010
"*Lacework Bridge*" © 2009
Originally appeared in Shelter of Daylight, April 2009
"*Night of Stars*" © 2008
Originally appeared in Aoife's Kiss #33, June 2010
"*Story Time in Pit City*" © 2002
Originally appeared in The 5th Di… March 2010
"*Until the Wind Changes*" © 1998
Originally appeared in Electric Velocipede #13, 2007
"*Cold Comfort*" © 2011
Originally appeared in The 5th Di… September 2011
"*The Sound of Wind in Wires*"
Originally appeared in Aoife's Kiss, September 2011

**Monstrosity Ink**

# Contents

*Snowfall on the City came about when two ideas met and mingled with an image from what I believe was an article on holiday shopping. The picture showed a couple heading down a city street toward warm, lighted windows on a blue, cold evening. The shops were pouring light out onto the sidewalks and snow was falling, and the lighted shopping area on the street was surrounded in a brighter bubble of colors than the rest of the picture, which looked cold and dark.*

*Whatever the intent of the photo — Christmas shopping during the recession? Commerce is the way to beat back the mid-winter blues? Merry Christmas? — the image combined the ideas of what if something you'd lost was still out there to be found ... if you could only figure out how? — with the idea of time travel, which routinely hurts my head. This story is the result.*

## Snowfall on the City

The city in the morning. Dark, quiet. From the iron stairs of the fire escape Erica can see the far horizons. Snow on the mountains. Crows wheel overhead, complaining. The sun seems dark but the air is fresh and wet.

She sighs and closes her eyes and in that moment she can feel the city change around her. Dawn ascent completed, the city drops its facade. She hears the voices of her neighbors raised in ongoing disagreement, voices of taxis locked in perpetual gridlock. When she opens her eyes the mountain will be the tenement next door. The snow will become soot or ash or fallout– she doesn't care which anymore. They tell you not to go outside but sometimes she has to. When she opens her eyes the cries of crows will resolve into the endless buzz of peacekeeper drones and provgov clean up crews. When she opens her eyes her choices will be tenth floor suicide or coffee.

Erica opens her eyes. The tenement across from her is dark and empty, burned out from just above her level. Gutted. Destroyed. Overhead she sees one single bird. Everything else is spy drones endlessly circling, suspicious, lurking.

She climbs back through the window where Mark is holding court. His face twisted and angry, he is explaining quantum theory to the stove which no longer works except when they put logs in it. He threatens the thing with the frying pan he holds and Erica gentles it away from him. He'll waste good food if she doesn't. Lately he insists he needs to feed the garbage disposal and since the thing no longer works she's tired of scooping gray, wasted food out of it.

When she tells him the garbage disposal isn't alive, he cries.

She's stopped telling him these sorts of things.

Everyone needs their own fictions anymore.

The city in the morning glistens with promise. Light blinds from unbroken windows. The sound of car horns is the promise of economy and progress. If she tries hard enough she can pretend the promise will be met. If she tries, she can believe Mark still teaches and the air doesn't burn and the ash and soot is snow.

But dawn only lasts an instant.


When Erica lets her guard down, when she slips up and stops concentrating for even a second, that's when her father's able to slide in and see her. She hates that. She knows he's not really there. He can't be. Her parents were in rural Pennsylvania when the war hit. Stupid war that shouldn't have worked, so many variables but everything The Enemy threw at them worked– biologicals destroyed crops and livestock, viruses ravaged cities, dirty bombs took out power grids and populations.

The nuclear strikes almost seemed like afterthoughts.

Like overkill.

Erica knows her father isn't really there. Even Mark knows her father isn't really there. But she's too tired to stop him once he's appeared. Everyone needs their own fictions these days but she doesn't understand why she needs her father. He's just as mean as he was in real life.

"When are you coming out to visit, Mouse?"

She hates that name. "Why do you call me that?" She's not tiny anymore. She works out. She trains. She still runs outside, through the now-deserted parks. The parks have been tumbled and tossed. Warheads turned the parks into obstacle courses, toppled trees, contaminated the water and killed every bird in the city. They say you should never exert yourself outdoors, especially without wearing a HEPA mask or some such. Erica runs anyway because during her runs the city is hers and she isn't afraid anymore.

Her father shrugs about the nickname. "Come stay with us for a little while. Do us all some good."

He looks almost kind. He can, sometimes.

"I can't, daddy. It's not there anymore."

So many people gone in a heartbeat; so many chances to say goodbye taken in a flash. She covers her face with her hands and when she looks up again finally her father is gone. Erica breathes a sigh of relief. She has to get ready for work. Provisional government's have assigned all remaining citizenry to CGG – Common Good Goals – teams in exchange for housing them in the remaining structures (which they announced they owned not too long after the initial blasts took out most of the structures) and food (which they confiscated promptly in order to leverage the cooperation of the public at large and without any sort of likely cover story.) Erica is a Scavenger. It is her job to crawl into buildings declared Safe (or at least Safe Enough) to bring back anything useable. She can spend up to a week in the simplest building. There's no real hurry. Buildings with really useful tools– food, medical supplies, communications– were ransacked even before The Homeland Defense: Recovery Team initiative could be formed. Buildings with food are already held. Buildings with medical supplies and drugs are in the hands of the gang bangers who made it through The Fall just fine, and even seem to be proliferating.

Scavenger's not a bad assignment– there are many, many far worse. Sewer workers, now in the throes of a cholera epidemic and held without recourse in a municipal center, worked till they die, recruited from the most desperate masses, their families receiving portions of their food and housed somewhere else. Somewhere Safe, or at least Safe Enough. Diggers, on corpse detail.

Erica doesn't care. Maybe Scavenger isn't so bad but it's still the worst part of her day. Too many bodies, too many parts. Too much death around her to report back to the Diggers and she hates leaving Mark alone; he's not all right anymore. Too cold in the city as November wends its way down, too many hours before she can return to the apartment and climb with shaking legs until she stands on the roof to watch the sunset, incredible displays of vermilions and salmons, of emerald and jade and midnight blue, fallout's gift to the city.

Too many hours of staring Reality in the face, without her own fictions to protect her.

Mark is quiet when she goes. He has finished with the stove for today, no longer talking quantum physics that daily sound more skewed to her uneducated ears. But when she kisses him goodbye he is with her, present in his own eyes. He looks at her with love and tells her to wear her coat and gloves and hat and scarf because it's cold out there today. He doesn't understand why it's so cold. Erica kisses him and thinks maybe she can bring him back a present. They're coming up on Christmas. Maybe she can find something to bring back.

Maybe she'll make it back home to him, she thinks, and she is out the door.

"You okay there?"

Cheerful voice out of the darkness. Erica clings to it and gropes her way toward the source of the light. Flashlight, one of the few remaining and as she gets closer she recognizes the face in the glow. Another Scavenger, one of her teammates.

"Yeah, fine. Thanks." Her heart rate is slowing a little but she can still feel the sweat cold against her forehead and she knows he's seen her panic.

"Break time, isn't it?" He's tall and slender, wearing a stocking cap and a puffy vest and when he puts the flashlight down he rubs his hands together against the cold.

"Is it?" She hasn't been able to find a working watch. It could be any time at all, so dark in the basement of the office building. Nothing here but firelighters– boxes of stored documents no one is ever going to need again.

"Luke," he says as if he knows she doesn't remember and Erica nods and says her name, though she's fairly sure he did remember. Cheap metal filing cabinet buckles when she leans against it and Luke looks closely at her. "You need to get up top for a while."

"I'm okay," she says but he shakes his head.

"You're panicked," and he takes her hand and at that point she truly is. Alone since The Fall, except for Mark, and they hadn't been that close before, just friends, neighbors. She stays with him because he's someone to talk to and because protecting him makes her feel safer and because taking care of someone gets her slightly better rations, when Mark doesn't feed them to the garbage disposal or the stove.

She twists her hand back out of his and takes a step away. Nothing is how anything used to be and stealing food or medical supplies is dealt with more harshly than rape or even murder. Luke blinks but doesn't move.

"Are you hungry? Do you want something to eat? Have you eaten today?"

She nods, doesn't trust herself to speak. She doesn't tell him she threw it all back up when she found the first body of the day, death dark features, hemorrhage and dried foam on his lips and eyes that stared past death and into her soul and asked why she had made it and he had not.

Luke starts to say something and she bolts. Curving blackness of the basement opens before her, faint light in the stairway, daylight above, gray and close and frozen but still light. By the top of the stairs she can't breathe. Gutted office building, lobby with the broken, twisted reception center. Blackened beams hauled out of condemneds to stand the upper structures. Erica runs for the door, triple thick, glass and chrome, cracked but intact since the Fall and beyond that the frozen November street, she just has to get her bearings and catch her breath and she'll find her team leader and ask to be topside the rest of the day. Tomorrow. Tomorrow it will all be all right again. Across the lobby, over buckled and melted decorative tiles. She hits the glass doors at a run and bursts onto the street and directly into—

Christmas.

Dead stop. She goes completely still.

Snow blankets the sidewalks, falls gently across twilight pale skies. Dry, light snow, not yet city-slushed, still white and pristine. Erica looks up and snowflakes fall on her face, cold against eyelashes and nose and lips. She licks her lips involuntarily, shudders at something she can't quite remember. She holds her hands out and laughs up at the sky and that's when she sees the wreaths on the streetlights, city's flags and greens and lights, red-and-white striping up the metal posts, holiday festive. Every year Mark laughed at her for finding the city's efforts attractive.

No, not Mark, and she bites down on that thought fast.

Two more steps and she's on the snowy sidewalk. Music plays from speakers hidden into wreaths and wired into light posts. People surge around her wearing trenchcoats and hats. Their noses are red with cold, their hands bundle packages against their chests as they struggle to keep their coats pulled closed against the snow and Erica strolls among them holding Jon's hand, gloved fingers overlapping, arms swinging together and both of them carry modest packages. They're happy just to be together in the deep evening outside the stores.

It's like a snowglobe. Snow curves into streetlights' glow as if falling from a glass dome over their heads. Erica can feel the heat from Jon's hand through her gloves and his and everything has gone quiet, the city fallen away because there's only the two of them. Taxis still blat and blare, people call, sidewalk Salvation Santas ring bells but they are safe and close and quiet together.

Beautiful, perfect winter's evening. Christmas shopping in the city with the man she loves.

If only something wasn't nagging her, the feeling she's forgotten something, something she doesn't want to remember.

"Are you all right, love?" Jon asks and she stops and pulls him tight to her, fierce embrace, almost fear. His arms go tight around her in return but she hears him laugh quietly into her hair. "What's this for?"

"Just in case," she tells him and when enough other people have bumped by them on the sidewalk she pulls back and laughs at his snow-capped hair and takes his hand again. They move toward home, the apartment they share with a view of nothing much other than the building next door but she pretends it's mountains and he's there and that's all that matters. At home there'll be hot chocolate and dry socks, because her feet feel cold and wet, and she turns to say, "Let's catch a cab—"

— and walks out of the moment and back into reality.

Luke's hair is full of snow. Erica frowns and reaches up to brush it away, half laughing, but she can't remember now how she knows him. Luke catches her hand and stops her and Erica shudders, suddenly aware of the low sky and the dark sun and the ash in Luke's hair.

When she stops moving he releases her hand.

"Where were you going? Someone said you just walked off the site."

When she looks around they're on the cracked and fallen sidewalk outside the department stores. She starts to speak and her voice isn't there. She puts her hand up against her throat and her eyes prickle with tears.

"You shouldn't be out here without a mask," he tells her and takes her hand, same way he did in the basement of the ruined office building.

"Neither should you," Erica says, but this time she doesn't pull away.

Quantum – a very small, indivisible, quantity of energy.

Physics – the science that deals with matter, energy, motion and force.

*Yes, Mark, yes, all right, even the stove has got it by now.*

Waking with a sinking feeling because she's missed dawn, first time since she discovered the way those instants of sunlight recreated the city. Waking with the memory of the night before. She'd cried and Mark had held her for as long as he could, but in the end she ran, made the roof and stood on the edge, ten story flight to the pavement below and it looked soft, snow covered pillows to fall forever into, sleep forever, no pain. No memory. Mark caught her hand and pulled her back and when she rounded on him he was already crying, big dark eyes and tears across his cheeks. He cried like a child, open and unashamed.

"What happens to me if you go? Huh? Who stops me from feeding everything to the garbage disposal or giving away whatever's here because someone asked?" He stared at her where she teetered on the brink, his grip on her hand both steadying her and making her more determined. "Don't be so selfish," he said before she got the chance to.

She stood unsteady against the edge and when her body shook close to falling she trusted him to hold her. Down on the sidewalk concrete disappeared under snow. Or fallout. Or whatever it was the city wept.

That day there's no sun at all, just endless cold and gray. Mark is lucid in the morning. It's a day he can come with her, probably. He isn't lecturing appliances or holding frustrated conversations with the faucets. He cooks breakfast for her – canned mushrooms, a couple eggs – luxury – very carefully, sprinkles hoarded Parmesan over it. They share a plate of it and coffee. Always coffee. It's not really the end of the world because there's still coffee. But it feels like it and she tries not to think about what happened the day before as she slides into coveralls and a bright orange vest, Scavenger clothes.

Mark is put on a digger crew, and Erica given a partner to work with and they're topside today, some street level building she can't even identify yet, maybe a shop of some kind, maybe a restaurant. She'd like to get a restaurant, find food. Provisional government trashes stuff like bacon, goes on and on about contamination and plastic and so on and Erica figures anyone taking their chances by still being alive can stand the risk of a few more contaminants. She found a pack of bacon a couple weeks ago and she and Mark shared it with the quarreling couple downstairs who came up when they smelled it.

Supervisor's a black chick with braids and mascara and who the hell bothers anymore? Name's Tanya and she's nice enough but one of those provgov newbies can't get enough of hearing herself take command and if she talks much longer they're going to lose what light they have so Erica slips away through the doors into charred remains and there's another Scav already inside, her partner, then, nods at her and they work silently together. It is a restaurant, spindly mutilated white painted metal chairs, tables upturned, shattered, burned. Light doesn't matter so much here— boarded windows, Provgov efforts to ensure every Scavenger is one of theirs. But skylights and there's precious little to see inside, the diggers have been through, burial detail, the bodies are gone and with them any chance of coats or shoes or watches. Fine by her, she's had enough bodies.

The two of them head into the kitchen, broken skylights overhead light the way and right now it is snow, not ash, not fallout, just snow, still white and frozen and powder slick. She looks up and the other Scav – long hair pony tail, girl not far off Erica's age – grins without saying anything, stoops down and wads snow and it's stupid, they'll make it melt, get wet and even colder, but Erica swoops down too, hard pack of white in her mittened hand, they throw at the same time, thud and fine spray explosion of snow across her face when the snowball hits her shoulder and the other girl laughs. Erica's missed and she's fast, ducks down again, forms the missile, lets fly and ducks return fire. Their laughter frosts and fogs in the room. They take refuge behind fallen ornate white iron tables, cry insults and havoc and laugher and the snow crunches under their feet and tracks with prints erratic and irresponsible and the light slides a fraction across the sky before they stop to breathe and laugh and move back into the kitchen, sharing out things the government supervisor will trash, bringing out cans of vegetables and fruits and condiments and meat, body back there in the walk-in freezer the diggers missed but Erica can almost bear it today.

They leave the restaurant together and neither has told the other her name. Erica wonders whose role she played in the Scav girl's fiction.

On the sidewalk again, suddenly nothing more she wants than to get away. Tanya is pulling another team together, wants them to go back in based on what's still there. Erica has packs of bacon and dried real mushrooms and actual meat in its USDA plastic hard against her spine. It's enough and she'd rather do anything but go back in. When she looks away from Tanya the world ripples for just the smallest instant, like an uncertain projector, a badly run film. There's something just in front of her now. The air turned hard or too bright. There's a pinprick hole in the bleached out sky, a very small, indivisible quantity of energy, or maybe the absence of it, the absence of anything there, a tiny black hole forming in her field of vision. Matter, energy, motion, force. She reaches out to touch it and her arm slides into the non-spot in the air, again that shifting change of everything she's viewing and then, at a distance, she sees the streets change, like an image in a crystal ball, a hologram, a dream. From a distance she can see the crowds, people moving, lights and greenery and she hears Christmas carols. She hears Tanya right beside her, saying something, some need or want or desire, and moves away without thinking or responding, and steps through the hole and back into the world.

"Where the hell were you?" he asks and he's looking right at her, that kind of relief that makes you feel angry for having been afraid.

This time she has no answer. City sidewalks, holiday decorations, end of November, past Thanksgiving, thick of the holidays but in that holding pattern between Thanksgiving and whatever holiday comes next, all of them later in the month. Plenty to do this time of year, preparations and parties, and still that sense of anticipation crossed with the frantic feeling of too much and too little time. She used to love this time of year, planning surprises for Jon, they held a party every year, guest list by whim, whoever they wanted, whoever could come.

Jon staring at her and she has no ready answer. Nothing comes to mind. Something is nagging at her and she's afraid to turn around like there's something behind her, some kind of childhood monster and it can't get her if she doesn't turn around. If she doesn't acknowledge it.

Jon's lips are cold when she kisses him. His initial surprise gives way and he hugs her, body warmth and white plume kiss, their breaths together. "I love you," she says, in case the moment gets away, and he laughs and kisses her nose and says he does too and he hasn't gone away. When she takes his arm and moves up the street beside him, her back to whatever it is behind her she fears.

They round the corner and she's shaken, startled, light too dark and sky too low and walking back into the Provgov Scav op, Tanya and her braids and the others in bright orange vests against the low gray sky. She looks back over her shoulder in time to see the lights and greens and city wink out but it's okay.  She's getting the idea now.

Mark isn't all right the next morning.  When she comes down from the roof, when the mountains have turned back into broken buildings and the sun's fire subdued by the ancient gray winter light, he is feeding the garbage disposal. Gruel, this time, she's hidden the foraged meat until he's all right again.  And when she squints Erica can imagine what he's doing, feeding it so carefully as if he spoons food into an infant's mouth.  Mark and Carol were new parents early fall and she can almost see the small face, bright worried blue eyes.  Mark's baby had seemed doubtful about Mark the few times Erica had seen her.  Mark himself had no doubts. Erica's eyes fill and she watches the gentle way Mark spoons rice cereal into the lifeless mouth of the garbage disposal and she imagines the little girl and doesn't step forward or say anything or interfere.  Everyone needs their own fictions these days and when she looks past him around the kitchen at sink and stove and dead refrigerator and useless dishwasher she can almost imagine a college class, a bunch of students, almost believe Mark's world of physics and lectures, but she has her own world waiting for her and she has to find a way inside.

She can't tell any more if it's snow on the ground or ash. It's like reality is blurring, fading away, and she has no interest in chasing after it– what has reality done for her lately?  There's Mark, of course, but he's retreating into his own bubble or pocket, his own fiction he's created.  If she could see it right, see into Mark's snowglobe, she'd see his fiction become reality.

If she can find a way.  To make her own story truth.

---

Today her partner is a middle aged woman as surly as she is fat and with improbable red hair that makes Erica realize some people are going to consider finding Miss Clairol as important as finding the next meal. The redhead has nothing to say to Erica and that's fine with her because she's not really here to Scavenge today. Today she's looking for a way to go home.

Different supervisor for Scavengers today and no clue where Tanya went. That's how Provgov works, moves people around like pieces in a board game, like somehow this will convince people that Provgov is on top of things and knows what it is doing. Like saying "you go here and you go there" is taking control and bringing order and getting things under control.

First drop's a bust. Place has been raided, picked clean, even the government's plywood carried off by looters and no one can spare tech to track them. Little store, and there's still stuff inside but nothing supervisor thinks is important. Next up is another office building and Erica does not want to be upstairs but she wants to be underground even less. Mostly she's just waiting for break time. December 1, definitely a shopping day. If she tries hard enough she might be able to remember the little boutique next door, the way it was, but that hurts too much and if this doesn't work she's going to have to stay here and keep Scavenging.

At least until she figures it out.

So she follows the sullen redhead into the office building, upstairs, redhead's panting by the third floor which is why she declares it the optimal floor for her to search. Erica says she'll head all the way up, work her way down, they'll meet in the middle. The other woman doesn't even bother to respond.

Out the door into the staircase and she makes a big show of running up a couple flights and then silence, back down as if this other woman has any sort of authority over her but she's still scared, so afraid it won't work.

So longing.

Back out on the street, the supervisor and her crew are about a block away, facing away from where Erica wants to go. She doesn't hesitate but turns and walks fast in the opposite direction. Provgov has certain restrictions, demands, expectations— largely, if you want to eat you work in some capacity for Provgov, and if you piss them off too much you might as well move somewhere else. They say they're just getting things set back up, but it seems a whole hell of a lot like martial law. So it's best not to be seen taking off from whatever your supervisor told you to do if you don't want to get moved to some worse detail.

She stops just beyond a cluster of city trees, trunks grown thick from their years here, leaves blighted by winter and by the Fall. She imagines the transition period, dawn, when the city lives and breathes around her and the ancient mountains stand. Hidden behind the trees she trembles on the edge of understanding, fights to create what before has only just <u>been</u>.

City streets in front of her remain torn and blasted and she forces her eyes open wide, searches for the clarity, the spark of change, that moment when the air hardens and sharpens.

There was nothing there.

*Why then?* she asks. *Why those moments?*

She closes her eyes against the rubbled asphalt and dead

city streets, pastes images of Christmas city in her mind, but that's only imagination, fiction above and beyond those moments of transition and she opens her eyes again and the city is still there, torn and blasted, but the idea is there as well.

She thinks of standing on the roof, alone up there because so many are afraid of the sifting ash and distant sun, and because so many are gone. And she thinks of the city in the morning, the way it stretches out above her when she stands up and out and free (closer to the fallout?) She thinks of the blurring and clearing and sudden dance of Christmas streets and shoppers and lights, the air hard and clear when she was here (closer to some of the sties of detonation, closer to epicenters.) Closer to the force and energy and motion that had released a type of particle, or energy, or matter.

She thinks of the city in the morning. The city the way it had been. She thinks of Mark, patiently lecturing on quantum physics, patiently reaching out to a family left behind.

She thinks of Jon.

Some distance ahead of her the air hardens, brilliant and clear like diamonds, and inside the snowglobe she sees flakes drifting down onto streetlights and shoppers and city streets. Behind her she hears someone call her name, sharp and angry; a demand. Ahead of her, inside the curve of time and space, under the dome of snowglobe, under the falling snow, she sees a familiar set of shoulders inside a familiar seedy trenchcoat.

She begins to run.

# Snowfall on the City

*I have no idea where this story came from. An image that has occurred more than once for me is that of enormous bridges, broken and rusting, obviously having collapsed years before. I imagine one level broken through, resting like a playing card or ramp from upper level bridge to lower level, and that the bridge is now used only by pedestrians and possibly people on bikes and motorcycles. This story seemed different as it was about the bridge itself rather than the bridge existing in the background. I believe this is the first story I sold to Tyree Campbell at Aoife's Kiss, who bought it for the annual collection, that year titled Shelter of Daylight.*

# Lacework Bridge

There's a bridge out of the city, off the island, and some night she's going to take it. At night city lights dot the edges of the bridge and light it like blue magic. By day it's nothing more than candy, decaying taffy in the sunlight. A falling conglomeration of steel and blue rust, of molten falling, like an old man's stomach gone soft. The lacework bridge was condemned half her lifetime ago, when rust-covered hex screws and chunks of angry, jagged steel and crumbling concrete started showing up in the bay, traced back to the river. Traced back to their island. The bridge was condemned and shut down and they were told there would be a new bridge soon, a beautiful bridge, something elegant yet direct. Some people were actually surprised as the months went on and no bridge appeared and the old one started tearing itself apart at night, every day more of the sparkling blue ocean visible under it until they had no choice but to condemn it themselves, leave it empty and unused and they started petitioning the mainland. They were still a part of the state (at that time.) They were still a part of the human race (then.) And they couldn't just be left out here to die, ships be damned, yes, they had boats but that wasn't the *point*, the point was that they'd been left alone out on their island in the green murk of setting suns and leaves and trees with the lacework bridge that every night twisted and broke. Now it resembled a strand of virus, now it looked like DNA, and the city lights from the mainland reflected off the blue steel. Every night Sophie watched the bridge, as she might watch a sleeping child breathe. Every night she dreamed of the magic that would allow her to cross the bridge.

Tonight there's gunfire from somewhere near the bridge. At first it's only the sound, not so unfamiliar in the night and nothing like the movies portray it, in real life (if that's what they have here) the sound of gunfire is a rapid popping, like giant blister packs opening or popcorn or something harmless. It's easy to become inured. It's easy to be lulled. Easy to walk unconcerned through the lush hot island night and more than one citizen has lost his life that way and more than one politician built endless droning campaigns on it.

Tonight she can see the gunfire, hot yellow flashes from down near the edge of the bridge, what she considers her dreaming place. Every night Sophie's been getting closer this past year or so, some hot young adult angst driving her because she knows she can't go (nobody goes) and she knows she can't stay (yes, you can, everyone stays, that's the way of it, her mother's voice in her mind like something stuck on replay.)

The stars overhead blink with the gunfire. Rapid on and off. Sophie sees it out of the corner of her eye and denies the knowledge for the impossibility it is. The heat of the night wraps around her, closer, the island closing in and the lights of the mainland spark magic against the night sky, on and off at the same time as the gunfire.

There's no moon tonight. There often doesn't seem to be a moon anymore. Sophie runs her hands up and down her arms briskly; the prickly heat's making her cold. The bell on the clock tower strikes– midnight, but she expects it to go on longer than 12 tolls. She leaves the street, cobbles under her feet (broken asphalt, so many times patched, petitions go nowhere anymore, even the most optimistic, hardheaded politician is finally figuring that out) and starts for home. At the edge of the stairs she kicks off her shoes so she won't wake her mother, avoids the stair that always creaks and crawls into her bed still dressed, her feet dusty black on the bottoms, hair salt tangled from the hot wind at the water's edge. She pulls the quilt up over her shoulder, suddenly sick with the heat, cold from it.

Her mother hears her anyway, comes in, a thick shadow with aching footsteps, sits on the edge of her bed without speaking and Sophie hears it all anyway.

*Don't go, please. You won't leave, will you? Not the way your father did–*

or her sister, or her aunt, or any of the others who have maybe gotten away from this place and maybe only fallen into memory, lost somewhere on the bridge.

Somewhere between pretending to sleep and being asleep her mother slides away.

The next day at the shop she starts hearing rumors. Tall, lanky Luke, his boney nose and floppy bangs and the way he moves as if somehow left behind by his own body and always struggling to catch up. Luke's one of the conspirators, back corner whispering that breaks off as soon as she appears, then starts up again.

At first she's a little nonplused; everything they're talking about seems a little non-starter, a little pointless. Have you noticed there's fewer boats? (Who hasn't?) Did you hear about the shootings? (Which ones?) And there's always rumors of No More Coming, of Care Flight ambulances that never came, of boat shipments never received.

Only now, something is different. Luke looks over Sophie's shoulder, repeatedly. The other two, the other shop clerks, like the island's bookstore needs four of them, everyone who's anyone and anyone who reads long since stopped coming in, having read every book and turned the shop effectively into a lending library and when was the last shipment of books received? But the other two, dumpy Pris and startlingly handsome— and gay— Kris, they're looking around too.

And "It's just rumor," she says, low voice, leaning closer as the paranoia reels her in.

"Not anymore," Pris says. "Haven't you noticed? Nothing's coming in." Her little bowstring mouth tightens up, smoker's radius extending off, like an offended cat's whiskers.

"Things are changing," Kris nods. Sophie forgets from time to time how unendingly stupid he is.

But Luke's nodding agreement. "Haven't you seen the bridge?"

She shakes her head impatiently. Gunfire near the bridge for how many nights now? But that's been going on since the lacework bridge was condemned, people rioting for food when their pantries were still full and okay, maybe things are a bit leaner now, but—

"It's pulling away," Luke says into her thoughts. "Stretching thinner and thinner."

"Or we are," Pris adds. "The island."

"We're moving?" Suddenly she's dizzy. She grew up here, and the bridge, it's only been half a dozen years but she's gotten used to it, to the mainland being the goal of everyone her age, to people growing up and going away and she's only been waiting her turn after all, for her mother to understand, to maybe even come too, there's nothing here anymore, this place is—

"Forgotten," Kris says, and she nods.

After work she heads down to the bay. It's been a good day at the shop, they sold three books and only returned two. They used to take turns ringing up purchases but the cash register's been broken for months so now they just write everything down on legal pads with rulered columns. It doesn't matter — by now everyone is just exchanging the same money anyway. Everyone on the island knows it; no one talks about it. Just before Sophie left high school for good her economics teacher asked for an example of a stagnant economy. Sophie had raised her hand and said,

"Our island," and her teacher gave her an F.

There's no gunfire tonight near the bridge, just the sound of tired metal. Sophie sits in her dreaming place, a little stone-crumbled alcove of rough concrete, edge of some abandoned building. The sun warms her as it sets, shines over her head and lights the lacework bridge from blue to mauve to gold to blue again. There's no gunfire tonight (too early? Too windy?) After a while she stands and sticks her hands in her pockets and goes down to stand at the water's edge beside the bridge.

The bridge leans out over the waves, insanely high arc up towards the deep purple sky. Metal has twisted in snowflake designs, the lacework bridge. She stands almost exactly opposite the base of it, the crumbling tortured infrastructure that links solid (island) land to steel (aerial) land. From her point of view the bridge looks like one of those hanging, twisted skeletons of a dinosaur, maybe one of the flying predators, because do they hang the non-flying ones from wires, don't they? Or is that only the ones that flew? But the bridge looks like the spine, seen from tail end, all those vertebrae, each leading to the next, up and up, twisted and uncertain and fragile and somehow natural.

Sophie blinks and it is only a bridge again, a bridge that looks as if it's gone through a war (rumors of war) and she traces the fretwork along to the city, picking out the familiar wharf signs, the lobster restaurant, the diner dives, the raft rental places, the snorkel place, the shops that sell useless souvenirs and tonight she can't read the signs. She can see the glowing neon box, orange letters that mean OPEN, in the diner window, but she can't actually read the sign tonight.

*It's late. It's almost dark.*

The island is pulling away, Pris said earlier. The way the bridge seems to pull thinner and thinner and have you noticed there's fewer boats?

"But there's one now," Sophie says out loud into the too-quiet night and she raises her hand to wave, but the men in the boat are standing, mirrored glasses over their eyes despite the darkening light, rifles propped on their hips. Each has one leg up on the side of the boat, some kind of macho, threatening pose. It works. Sophie drops her hand and watches the boat slide silently out of sight, past the curve of the island.

There are riots for food. That's what she knows. They grow a lot of their own food here. Import what they can't grow. The rioters are only frightened. Everything is all right, and it's riots for food and sometimes gangs, that's what the gunfire at night around the bridge is. She grew up here. She knows this place. That's all it could be.

That night her mother makes hamburgers and hamburger buns, precious flour spent on a yeast experiment. There's mangos and oranges and pie for dessert. Sophie helps set the table and they talk about her mother's card game with the neighbors and Sophie's day at the shop and she doesn't say anything about the boat she saw tonight, still trying to decide if she should when she looks up and her mother is crying.

"I want you to go," she says, before Sophie can say anything, before she can even scramble to her feet. "It's time. It's past time. It's getting to be too late."

As if to underscore her words, there's gunfire, late tonight but there, distant, maybe from the bridge. "You're young, you can get out, and if there's any way to send anyone back, then maybe–"

"I'm not going without *you.*" She's angry, instantly, not panicked or afraid or sad, just angry. All this time she's stayed, all those nights her mother had begged, aloud or with her eyes– don't leave me, don't go. I'm not young anymore and I don't have anyone else. This, now, seems like betrayal. *I've waited all this time, been here for her, I know there's a life out there–*

And she knows, without knowing, without admitting she knows, that it would have been easier to get to it before. Before the boats stopped coming. Before the other boats started coming.

"You have to," her mother says. "I can't get across the bridge. There isn't any other way."

Sophie stands in the middle of the kitchen. The air still smells like hamburgers, like betrayal. "How can you ask me to–"

"There's no other choice."

It's hard to say good-bye to people when you can't even admit that you are going because going by itself may be illegal. But she tries– Kris and Pris and Luke are as close to friends as she has on the island. She tells them she is going to take a few days off (no one does this: what is there to do here?) And that she wants to see some different water (as if that makes any sense, as if the other side of the island was any kind of adventure, even if it is a different city.) After she's gone, safely gone, Luke can explain it to Kris. Currently he just looks confused as Pris hugs Sophie and cries a little and wishes her a "good vacation."

From her dreaming place, she watches the sunset flow

across the lacework bridge. Her heart pounds hard against her ribs, has for hours. She hasn't seen any boats, at all, only a few sail boats out by the mainland, just dots of white now where once she could read adverts on some sails, catch the colors the sailors wore. The bridge grinds in the light wind. There's the sound of tortured metal, the creaking of supports. She hadn't realized she'd come to understand it as the sound of freedom.

When night falls in earnest, she shoulders her pack. Her mother made it, because there weren't any black packs on the island to buy, and because ordering such a thing would take so long and other people would know about it.

Making this one must have taken a long time, too. Sophie understands this. Her mother has been planning Sophie's escape for a while.

*Then why those nights, saying the same thing? she wonders. Why the 'don't leave me, please stay, you're all I have'?*

But her mother hasn't said it in weeks. Months. Sophie's only heard it anyway.

All the while she was making the pack, black on black, or navy blue, she'll blend into the shadows on the bridge, as long as there are no flashes of gunfire.

*And the stars going on and off, as if they're not real anymore, she thinks. As if they're not real. Or as if we're not.*

It's full dark now. The lights across the bay in the city spark a magical glow against the night sky. Wind whistles through the lacework bridge. Steel groans and settles. There is no sign of a boat anywhere.

All the time she's been hidden she's imagined herself sneaking out, stealthy as a spy in a thriller, her back to the wall, that funny foot-over-foot sideways movement actors effect in thrillers that seems to indicate they've become invisible. All of it ridiculous, because there is no wall for her to slide along, only a large empty expanse of dockside, island wharf outside the empty shops, maybe 50 feet of empty space where people used to walk in the sun, talking and eating ice cream.

Plus she'd trip over her feet if she tried that sideways thing.

At last she just takes a step. One first step. Then another. And nothing happens. No alarms sound. No one shouts. The night doesn't get any darker; spotlights don't light her up. She doesn't run. She's been down here plenty of times at night, dreaming in her dreaming place. Admittedly then she wasn't dressed in black from head to toe. Still.

She crosses the expanse between her dreaming place and the lacework bridge. The first few feet of bridge are still whole but she can see where the bridge is tearing loose from the island.

All those hours spent plotting what it would be like to cross the bridge. Before everything happened, of course, she had crossed it plenty of times, driven to the mainland in search of trendier school clothes or because she couldn't wait the additional week or two for the newest CD or video game or book to make it to the island. She's walked the bridge before as well, just like everybody has this side of the island, gone out to fish or just to look, walking halfway to see how home looks from there or watch the sun set. Since everything began she's sat and watched the bridge, imagined where each and every step would take her. She's crossed this bridge a thousand times; this is only the first time.

The bridge groans under her weight. Structural steel shakes in the slight breeze off the water. Her quads strain to pull her up the first couple huge steps onto the bridge itself. The sound of steel shivering is enormous. She looks around but doesn't see anyone on the water and she doesn't look behind her yet.

The first 30 feet or so is nearly straight up. Across from her, the bridge slides up more gently, the "other side of the road," but she's going out, not coming in and despite being on foot, despite the bridge being deserted, it seems important. Her leg muscles protest, dragging her upward. Something in the middle of the bridge has let go, broken in half for her to climb up like this. She holds the thick cables along the guardrails, pulls herself hand over hand. Full dark now, but beneath her feet she can still see the water, far below, black but catching light from the mainland.

The night wind catches her face, tangles her hair with salt, chaps her skin. Her mouth is dry before she's gone a third of the way. She hears the night around her, the familiar protests of the bridge, the wind, the sound of life from the mainland.

The gaps in the bridge grow larger, like tears in lacework. Once she stops utterly, watching a boat glide silently under her feet. She wonders if it's anyone she knows, someone getting out, home-built boat from somebody's garage. Until she sees the lights from the mainland glint off the weapons.

When its gone she starts again. Her heart still pounds futilely against her. By now she's traversed the spinal tail of the dinosaur; the body rears up ahead of her. Sophie stops and stares back at the island. It's utterly dark. All those nights recently with the electricity flickering, iffy; tonight it's gone for good. When she looks back at the mainland– the glowing neon carnival colors, the faint sounds she can now hear– it looks like a party. Like life. Or the future. She looks back briefly at the island one more time. She's promised to send back help. If she can find it. She wonders if she will.

At halfway the bridge on her side– the "you are now leaving" side– is torn in half. The other side, Sophie sees, some five feet away maybe, is smooth and flat. There are a few holes in the base, not many. She starts to look back over her shoulder but there's nothing to see there and she stops herself. Below her, dark water. Ahead of her, mainland. It's not a hard jump. Maybe only four feet across, three feet down to the other side. Though the other side of the bridge, the one facing her, just <u>ends</u>, terminates; the torn end facing her is stable, smooth, level. It looks like cars could park on it and sit staring at the island and the torn and twisted sculpture that was once a bridge without making that side sag or fall. It can definitely support her weight.

Sophie backs up a little, preparing to run, gain some momentum before her jump. Just before she runs, she looks down through the lacework bridge and sees another boat gliding beneath her with men, and guns. She doesn't hesitate. She takes a breath, as if she's heading for the water, and she runs toward the edge of the lacework bridge.

Behind her in the night flashes of gunfire light the bridge sporadically. Overhead, the stars turn off, and on.

*Night of Stars was written at the height of the Great Recession when foreclosures and short sales were all over the news. During our own go-rounds with mortgage companies, which eventually were settled amicably for my husband and I (don't know how the mortgage companies felt), our mail lady would stop daily with a thick stack of communications from the mortgage company which, in crossing all T's and dotting all I's, wrote to us under every conceivable name, as a married couple and as individuals. So I got mail to Jennifer Rachel Baumer, Jennifer R Baumer, Jennifer Baumer, once, notably, to Rachel Baumer and once, even more strangely, simply to Jennifer, which made me feel rather Cher-like. These were all sent certified, return receipt requested.*

*The story that emerged from such hounding was written for a science fiction workshop where I'd been told to "push the envelope and take chances." I did, starting the story with an explicative I could well imagine mortgage companies eventually coming out with. That must have been too much and the story didn't win over the workshop leaders, but the rewritten version found a home in Aoife's Kiss.*

## Night of Stars

"Dear Moron. Get out."

Kevin rolled his head along the back of the squeaky porch swing gave her one of *those* looks. Flakes of paint from the metal swing frame already dotted his dark hair; he'd watched her pace before she opened the official foreclosure letter. "It does not say that."

"Might as well," Jessica said. She stood on the rickety wooden porch with the letter warping under her sweating fingers. Dusty sunlight struggled through the particulate cloud that had enveloped the planet after Near Planet Object asteroid Metallica had slammed into the Pacific, annihilating the polar bears and putting an end to the debates about global warming. Earth was now hot, dusty and dry.

It was also home. Jessica had spent a lot of time out in the stars, sailing between planets, surveying and charting routes and drill sites for mining companies. There were computers and unmanned ships that could do the same job, but mining companies sent geologists, tacked on the name astro-geologist and then paid them wages that were still cheaper for the corporations than computer ships. It didn't matter – the pay wasn't the point. Conquest was the thing for solar sailors. Tiny one-body ships, like the universe's smallest interstellar studio apartment. Jessica excelled at it, darting in and out of orbit around dying suns, using their light to propel her close enough to chart the minerals and mineables, dashing away again like a super-powered firefly.

She was good at it, but she'd never relaxed into it. There'd always been that edge of terror for Jessica, the blurred-vision, pounding-heart *How did I get myself into this?* type of panic. Now it had been a year since she'd been out there. Just the idea brought on the edges of panic. Her throat tightened. Her chest seized up. Asthma impaled her lungs.

"Breathe," Kevin said. He stood, the swing creaking behind him in the silent desert air. Not many people had stayed in the western states after the Night of Stars, as an unfortunate number of survivors now called the Decimation.

"How do you always know?"

"I can see your face. You go all still. You're never still."

She was still uncomfortable with anyone who understood her. Five years together and she was still uncomfortable knowing he could read her. One year since the Decimation and she wanted to be brave. Stoic.

She wanted not to wake screaming when she could feel the tail of her ship take the hit, feel the spin start, the heat of free fall through the atmosphere burning her. She'd come to her aunt's house because it seemed safe in the desert. Flat. Un-cratered. And at night she could see the stars, when she was brave enough to look up through the constant cloud cover. Out here city lights had never reflected back from the night sky, dimming the stars. And now there were very few city lights.

Kevin was still watching her. He was going to hug her if she didn't distract him. She was going to cry if he hugged her. Crying would solve nothing. Jessica squinted at the thick paper in her hands. "'Get out. You are no longer entitled to the plot of dirt you thought you bought. We never said it would be easy. We never said it would be fair. We just wanted' – "

"What does it really say?"

"'We just wanted your tax proceeds to finance our galactic hegemony' –"

"Jessica."

"Fine." She wrinkled her nose and drew a breath. The letterhead smelled rich, thick and cardboard-y, of fine offices on some distant planet and of secretaries drenched in perfume. No attorney had ever gone near this letter. It was a form letter, full of spite and venom and greed. On something resembling vellum.

"What's it say?"

"We regret to inform you we are looking into foreclosure proceedings on your property."

Kevin closed his eyes. "And?"

"'You and all your wastrel friends will be thrown off planet' – " But she stopped before he opened his eyes and said, "It's a letter of non-payment. Apparently they sent a lot of them to my Aunt before she died."

"And she just happened to not mention it when she sold it to you?" He leaned over and took the letter from her. It didn't seem to improve any when he read it.

Jessica thought about the other letter she'd received. The one still in her pocket. The one she hadn't told Kevin about. The "we want you back." The "get out of jail free" letter (or at least get out of debt.) The one from her old employer. Andrews. Not just ex-employer. Ex-lover from many years ago. Ex-. The one who said he wasn't going to give up, wasn't going to let her go that easy, and kept reappearing in her life.

"What else does it say?" she asked, distracting herself again.

"We've got until the 19th to make payments," Kevin read.

Jessica leaned her forearms on the paint-peeling porch rails and stared at the empty desert. The asteroids, Metallica and its much-smaller, splintered-off friends, had seemed pretty determined about hitting urban areas. Her aunt's property in Very Much Nowhere Nevada had been spared. Her aunt had owned a lot of acres, a vast spread of empty desert no one had wanted before Metallica.

Almost as vast and desolate as a star field. And everyone wanted it now. Rebuilding the cities would take time. So much devastation. As if bombs had gone off. It was faster, easier and more financially rewarding for banks and developers to first build in empty, unpopulated and unaffected areas, then take their time moving everyone back to the cities, at least those who were willing to go.

Her aunt's property would make the bank and the developers very happy.

"The 19th of what?"

He didn't respond right away, so she already knew what he was going to say. "June."

"That's next week," she said. Overhead rusty-sounding birds circled something unfortunate on the devastated earth. "Listen. They've already sent the vultures."

Kevin moved beside her and leaned one arm over her shoulders. "Those are crows, Jess."

She wasn't so sure.

It wasn't like it was a particularly nice house. It was square and squat and small. The paint was peeling everywhere there was paint. It had originally been gray and had somehow gotten dingier as the gray bleached white over countless desert summers and after the initial radiation blast from Metallica hit.

And it wasn't as if it were an old family homestead. She hadn't spent summers here with her aunt, running barefoot through the sage and catching lizards. She'd only come for single-weekend guilt-visits with her parents, who always seemed to think her aunt was up to something living way out here.

But when Aunt Rose died and Kevin was injured in the initial blasts and Jessica was – her mind veered away – after the Decimation, it became a haven. And when Aunt Rose died, it became Jessica's haven.

A haven mortgaged heavily to galactic banks which were in turn mortgaged heavily after Earth started needing funds to rebuild.

Kevin turned and looked at her and she shuddered. She always did, anymore. That frisson of cold that ran down her back. The familiar features, forever unfamiliar now. Just off. Smooth simulated flesh. Smooth simulated features. They'd mostly recreated the dark brows, the dark hair. The set of his mouth. The way he usually looked just about to smile.

But they'd missed a scar here, a wrinkle there. And the new body was aging and changing differently. She was never quite able to forget. When the ejecta thrown by the Decimation hit Reno, Kevin had been in one of the buildings that tumbled down. They'd barely gotten him out in time, in the wave of first rescues before the global nature of everything became clear and the authorities stopped actual rescue in favor of triage and recovery. And over the course of that first night, it turned out that *just in time* wasn't.

ReBodies were expensive. They were luxuries, ways to stay with loved ones past what the body said was possible. The new body was a haven for Kevin.

An expensive, heavily mortgaged haven. A haven legally tied to the house.

He put his arm around her in the hot, still afternoon, but his arm felt cold. She thought she could feel him tremble, just a little. Just what he couldn't control.

"We'll figure it out," he said. "I can do some moonlighting, get a second job." There was plenty of rebuilding to do. Survivors were spreading back out from the frightened packs they'd gathered into after the event.

Jessica put her head against his chest and nodded. "I'll

contact the bank, the attorneys. Ask for an extension. We'll figure it out," she said. Repeating what he'd said. Hoping to believe it.

Even now that carpenters were in demand it wouldn't be possible for a carpenter to pay those mortgages back down, not even with a second job. Not a carpenter in a repaired and fabricated body. The banks had them on the run now – high premiums, high penalties for being behind, high pestilence for having been in arrears. High petulance – and resistance – to their getting out. There was no way to win with small payments, even if they both got second full time jobs. It wouldn't be enough fast enough. Not with Jessica safely on Earth.

The mining companies were still expanding. Off-planet minerals for other human-populated planets. Iron for rebuilding. It was all in demand.

Solar sailing astro-geologist surveyors were in demand.

Jessica took the other letter out of her pocket and looked at it. The mining company's insignia stood out sharply on the white envelope. When she looked up, Kevin was looking at the envelope too. His gaze rose to meet hers. Slowly. He didn't look like he was about to smile.


Nights out here were long and dark. Used to be the night wind was cold and smelled of sage and transient desert moisture. Now the wind smelled burned, the way Earth did.

Among the stars her tiny one-person world would be sterile, clean and chemical. It was supposed to be safe again in near space. The band of Near Earth Objects had moved on. No more asteroids nearby.

That didn't mean they weren't out there where she ended up. She wasn't mapping mining possibilities on Earth's sun.

"You always knew they were out there," Kevin said.

Kevin's shoulder still felt the same. As if his surgeon had recreated the hollow where her head fit out of some blueprint when he remade everything. From where they lay on the bed she could see out a corner of the window where the curtain kept stirring in the night breeze. When it gusted into the room she could see the moon, three-quarters and fading. The same old moon in the newly designed sky – all the dust made it diffuse and uncertain.

The way Jessica felt. "Do you <u>want</u> me to go out there?"

"Of course not." He went up on one elbow and looked down at her. "We can figure it out, Jess. We can do something else. I'd rather."

She sat up with her back to him, her feet on the bedroom floor. They'd lose for certain if she stayed. They couldn't fight the bank. The global economy had reduced individual economies to less than trivial matters.

In her mind the ship closed around her again, the claustrophobic cockpit tapering into "living space" which was more office than anything else. The mining company didn't care about her living. The bank didn't care about Kevin living.

She could come back from the stars.

Kevin couldn't come back from foreclosure.


The launch ship was a weapons regrade. It could still be used to shoot asteroids out of space because, of course, that had worked so well last time. But the cruiser made a good carrier.

Jessica moved through the row of solar ships, her heart pounding twice as fast as her unwilling footsteps. Crew filtered in, other surveyors wearing modified spacesuits like

Jessica's – small, light, easy to move around in, made of something light and tough like the under-wrapping plastic used under siding on Earth houses.

She'd kissed Kevin goodbye at dawn the day before and joined the crew. They'd headed out of orbit, into space, heading for a nearly dead star. And she'd done everything she could to avoid Andrews.

*You read too much into things,* Kevin kept saying. *Like that letter. The foreclosure letter.*

The one that had started with her name. Her mortgage account number. Her husband's mortgaged body's account number.

*At least Andrews wants you back on his crew.*

She didn't tell Kevin that's what bothered her.

So far, so good, though. Not a sign of Andrews. Maybe he didn't want to see her either. Or maybe he just didn't know she was on his crew.

Or maybe he was standing across the bay from her, apparently oblivious to the hustle around him. He only watched her.

Now that she'd seen him it was pointless to pretend she hadn't. Jessica kept her eyes on him as he slowly oozed down the line of ships toward her. She couldn't figure out what had been wrong with her. What had she seen in him?

Andrews seemed to think the same thing. What had been wrong with her? He asked, and without waiting, added, "Good to have you back."

*On board,* Jessica finished his sentence. You mean *Good to have you back on board.*

But she didn't say anything. She smiled, noncommittal, and climbed into her ship. Just before she launched, she heard Andrews over her radio: "I told you I'd get you back.

How's that foreclosure coming? Must be just hell on Kevin."

Kevin and the new body. Andrews and the foreclosure he couldn't possibly know about.

That was paranoid thinking. *You read too much into things.*

Andrews smirked at her and patted her arm with proprietary smugness.

Jessica's stomach shuddered. With all her heart she didn't want to go out there. But she could imagine the forms they'd need to fill out, long, filled with legalese. The forms they would fill out after just a couple mapping runs, if she got lucky. Astro-geologists were in demand now. A couple trips and she and Kevin could fill out those forms, stating the mortgage was paid up. The foreclosure was called off. Long legal forms. Badly written instructions to go with. She'd make fun of the language. They'd make fun of it, together, and there'd be a together for them to be.

She set her sights on the stars and headed away from home in order to save it.

*In 2002 and the beginning of 2003 I made my only foray into having an office outside my house. I was hoping to branch out from magazine writing to client writing (a change that didn't happen for another couple years) and took a tiny office in a historic house along the Truckee River. The move did nothing for my finding clients (because I never told anyone I was there, and the potential clients I wanted weren't psychic, apparently) but in the process a friend gave me an old desk to use. Before the office was ready, the desk sat in what should have been the dining room (if we'd had a table there) in the rental my husband and I were living in. One Saturday morning when Rick was working and I was bored, I started doing some freewriting exercises. I ended up writing by hand for 88 minutes straight without stopping (that's how the exercise works, and why my hand no longer worked when I stopped). I'd written through four prompts and had the basis of a story called, at the time, Suicide Pit.*

## Story Time in Pit City

*Cassie*

This isn't the kind of city you make a mistake in. This is one scary place to live and mistakes cost lives. I'd heard about this place long before I ever decided to move here—everyone hears about this place. Most people don't decide to come here, though.

I'd run out of options. Born and raised in a hellhole on

the west coast where everything's supposed to be sunny and good and all that crap but there are still those small inbred towns you find anywhere else across the country, those places that are the underbelly of America and that's where evil blossoms.

I'd come here because you could make a killing in this city. If you were looking for money and didn't care how you got it, this was the place to be. But like I said, you don't go around making mistakes here and I'd made them. Too many of them. And now I was standing at the edge of the Suicide Pit and trying to decided exactly whether to stay or go and whether or not I really had any options any more.

"Stinks," the girl next to me said. There weren't a lot of people here today. Few workers down below, those sections sealed off and lights flashing around them. They were working in some of the deeper portions and it was kind of a pisser because that's where I was headed. If I was actually headed anywhere, that is. Like a lot of people, I'd come here to think. Paid a pondering charge, so to speak, and staked the deposit in case I made up my mind before leaving. God, this place. It was usually like this but the smell wasn't always so bad. Lots of times you could think better. Guess that's why they were cleaning up a portion.

Pit isn't just a pit. It's like a mile all the way around, with different levels for different intents. Time was advertising tried to compare it to Dante's nine circles of hell but that didn't really take. People thinkin' about visiting the Pit don't want to be reminded of Hell necessarily. So here I am, lookin' down. There's places here not so deep. Shit, there's a beginners leap (and a fine for using it, I might add.) The equivalent of a two story hop. For them maybe not so desperate as they like to think they are. And there's the ten story jump with the concrete stanchions studded throughout and hell if it doesn't look impressive but a few years ago they wired up some willing jumpers and figured out most of them were dead before they ever hit— heart attacks in mid-air. So all that pokey rebar and hardass concrete is just for show. If you're going to go out, may as well make it look bigtime, I guess.

"Nasty," I agree finally, looking at her straight on for the first time. (It's really considered rude to stare here unless you're 110 percent sure the person next to you is in Meditating Mode, Pondering Position, Thinking... whatever, you get my drift.) She looks like she's maybe 20 and that's probably giving her more credit than she has years. Can't figure out what somebody that age could have done to feel so bad about. And that's nonsense, of course, she could have killed somebody at age two for all I know. She could be gene altered intel so high my hesitation makes her want to give me a good hard shove. But she looks just like anybody else, not that slightly spacey pie-eyed look half the intels develop.

And me. You couldn't tell just by looking at me what I'd done that's brought me here. Of course I suppose she mighta lost somebody. People have all kinds of reasons to jump and ever since they repealed those stupidass illegal-to-kill-yourself laws, places like this have sprung up in all the best of the worst cities around the globe. I hear DC has a pit put this one to shame.

But I digress. She's just standing there like she's waiting for me to say something— another deviation in the etiquette that's formed around these places: don't expect anyone to come out of themselves. Let everyone alone. If conversation doesn't look mutual then— but WTF, it is mutual. She just looks young and helpless. And I only came here to think anyway. I turn toward her and before I can say anything she says, "My name's Sarah," and damned if that isn't one of the biggest breaches of etiquette, giving a name, making an introduction. People are anon, here. People– well, I've said why people come here. And before I really think about it I've said, "I'm Cassie," and there you are.

We end up sitting, legs swinging over the Pit. Sun comes out from behind a bunch of clouds grayer than the fresh ash in the Pit and it feels good on my shoulders, almost like a massage. Sarah reaches over and shakes my hand. "You're thinkin' today, aren't you?" Oh, this girl's just so not with the program but she's got that young vulnerable open face.

"Thinkin'," I nod and the sun shines and below us the cat digs up a fresh layer, broken limbs and vomit on that one, it's a distance but I can see where he threw up, still alive when he hit, that's the problem with the mid-height sections of the Pit. And then the sprayer comes along and coats the body for burn. There's ash starting to float upwards from the deeper ends and we're going to have to get out of here before much longer, it can get pretty unbearable when they flame. Stink, smoke, ashes. But there's no laws or health codes or anything here– that would be pretty stupid, wouldn't it?

I realize Sarah's asked me something and she's looking at me with those wide gray blue eyes. Don't know what the question was I missed but I can guess what it is she wants to know. "I ran out on some people who needed me," I tell her. "We were in a bad place at a bad time and it was their bad idea. But that doesn't excuse my leaving them behind."

It's all I can remember and more than I should be able to remember what with takin' a handful of Amnesics. More than I wanted to say, too. Sarah's quiet for a minute and I'm not lookin' right at her but off into the Pit where a woman's arm seems to be waving but it's just from the heat of the chemical fire.

"Who were they?" Sarah finally asks. Even though I wasn't looking at her, she sounds like she's been biting her lip, like she was afraid to ask.

"No one," I answer and then get up the guts to look at her again. "I made myself forget." But her face looks pretty damn familiar and her eyes are beginning to fill with tears. I haven't seen any articles on it, but I'm thinking family reunions are taboo here, too.

*Tish*

We went out last night, me and George and Sarah. Just a lark. Things have been so bad lately for Sarah we thought we better get her out of the house and get her mind off her troubles before much longer. So we took her to Throm, which is supposed to be the hottest nightclub ever yadda yadda yadda blah blah blah. But actually it is pretty cool. They've got a place out front, kind of a staging area, where you have to grease up before you go through the portal and they've got these yummy boys and girls who grease you. It's a total strip down and you really *want* them to grease everywhere because baby when you walk in you're walking through fire and if a part of you is unprotected– fsssst! or something like that. Anyway, I had this white haired little boy with a chest I could've spent an evening biting, just running my teeth over that alabaster. But what the hell, I'm way the fuck off track. We took Sarah there and were having a pretty decent time– redressed, redrugged and got the goop out of our hair and the music is mind splitting loud and everyone there is kinetic, no wall flowers, no as you please. This is a danceplace and people are dancing. And Sarah got into it and so did George and I was barhogging what the hell someone has to keep an eye on them in Pit City. It's not somewhere to let your guard down. And I turn away for maybe two minutes tops— just to order a blue toad and then to help the barguy catch it again— and when I look back again I can't see Sarah for shit.

Okay, yeah, fine, I know what you're going to say. Sarah's a big girl and she should be able to take care of herself just fine in a danceplace in Pit City. She got here on her own, didn't she? But that's just it. She didn't, really. Sarah came here chasin' somebody. She doesn't think I know it but I do. She was trailin' tailin' someone who ran out on her when the stakes got high. And she hasn't stopped looking since she got here. Only now I think maybe she has. Stopped looking. Because she's set on following somebody and she's pretty fucking intent. Looks like she knows just what she's about. Without thinking about it I signal George's personal comm system and head after her because she's almost to the door. By the time George catches up to me Sarah's keyed a cab and we have to wire ours over legal to catch up.

"Stay where she can't see you," I tell George and he says, "You think I don't know that?" But Sarah's attention is on the cab in front of her. We could be in her backseat— if the cab had a backseat— and she wouldn't know it. And when my attention does come away from the twisty path the two in front of us are following, it's to realize we're going deeper and deeper mid-city, inner city, inner inner city, the place where pit workers live and I don't mean those poor sods what are down there in amidst, cleaning and burning and bailing. I mean Pit Workers, those people who know how to find and manipulate the souls of our dearly departed, those blots on humanity who can take a jumped jumper and bring 'em back just to the point of life, not like they obviously hadn't had enough troubles given they've just taken a two to thirty story fall but now you've got a black magician making your soul into silly putty, opening up your spirit for the energy and trapping your still beating brain— so to speak— in a place where he can use it and you can't. It's like one of the most vile crimes in Pit City and that makes total sense and it's into the neighborhoods where these sorry sons of bitches live that Sarah's little cab is leading us, following whoever the hell it is she lit out after from the club.

I look over at George but his mouth is a solid line of upset and his eyes are trained no waver on Sarah. She ought to be able to feel us with George that intent behind her but when I turn back it's only to find that Sarah has moved ahead a little, staring forward, following, and we follow her. George, beside me, suddenly points, distracted for only a split second. "What's that thing over there?" he asks, pointing at a huge structure of iron and concrete. I don't know but I have a feeling we'll soon find out, because we're heading straight for it.

*Sarah*

The holding cells loom up in front of me. Kind of knew that's where we were headed the minute we left the pub. Danceplace. I'm so rattled now I'm not sure where I was. Only where I am. I've come this far and I'm not going to stop. I can't believe she was there, at that place, there big as life and she didn't see me. Don't know she'd recognize me if she did. Sure didn't at the Pit yesterday. Knew she'd grab onto the Amnesics after it all went down. Cassie never was one to handle those kinds of things. Look at the way she lit out of the holding cells. Yet here she is, back in Pity City, and I suppose I should feel sorry for her– poor little Cassie– all shook up– but she left me there to die. All there is to it.

The holding cells. My stomach lurches and Cassie's cab comes and goes in my line of sight just before the tears start in earnest. I don't have to see her though to follow her. She's under my skin, in my bloodstream. Just like I don't have to look to know the others are following me, George and Tish. Of course they are. But it's okay, they'll be safe. My attention is riveted on Cassie. My sister. And the events of three years ago.

Seventeen and on my own in the big wide world. Never thought my parents would sign the consents but I guess I'd worn them down with truancies and vagrancies and drug charges and then all the money in rehab and the rest of it. Worn them down and they signed and I was a free woman all of a sudden, both of them all at once, free and woman. And then comes Cassie, four years older and all knowing and wise and stay with me, I'll keep you safe, and when I told her what she could do with safe it changed over to well, then, let me go with you and what the hell– no reason she couldn't.

So we world hopped for a couple months and it was more jazzed having someone with me. Cassie knows when to party and she knows when to pull back and I know the first part of that and not even the meaning of the second but that's okay because when it got to that part for Cassie she'd bug the hell off and leave me to razor fucks or suck parties or the times we'd cocktail whatever anyone had brought and fuck tomorrow, medical science can all put almost anything back together and most of the new synthetics are illegal as hell and a helacious ride but there's no permanent dark doodoo dumped in your brain so what the hell, it's a ride, ride it. From SoHo to SF, Seattle to Singapore. To the Philippines and Manila where we partied in the rubble of the terrorist hit towers to NY again where we built monuments to the trade towers and fucked in rivers that glow in the dark. I know how it sounds. I know how I look. Wide eyed innocent with that blue gray gaze and the innocent don't-hurt-me mouth that just begs to be slapped and raped. But most of that had never happened until that night in Vegas when the rich guy's pregnant daughter shotgunned herself in the belly, ultimate protest over the last idiot Repubs rule overturning Roe vs. Wade and the Dems back in power but they've been a little distracted cleaning up the latest big-business-in-bed-with-big-government scandals and overthrowing the latest dictatorship in yet another small, unpopular, anti-US country and so abortions are on the no-no list and Shana, she couldn't take another drug addicted kid in her life, synthetics might not hook the mother but some naturals do and anyway syns play havoc with offspring. And no sooner had she put both barrels to and through her gut than daddy's men were with us, pissed off as all fucking hell and there to clean up the pieces, ghod, little bit of Shana here, little bit there, daddy the super lawyer was there minute his little girl's PCS went offline and we were all still there, highs abruptly terminated and stupid looks on our useless faces as ex-CIA now private cops poured into the courtyard and trussed us, plastic twist tie handcuffs, blindfolds, gags, masks, which was bad because I knew right then we were going to Pit City Kitty, chance to show daddy how woefully, deeply, personally sorry we were and make up for it then and there. Only I wasn't that sorry. Shana was kind of a bitch and my dying for her wouldn't bring her back to daddy dearest even in this day and age and I just wasn't into self immolation for a rich bitch mommy of spawn– how many now? and Cassie– that night she didn't have the sense to run, to turn in early, "I'll leave the light on for you, let me know when you get in," and she went along for the ride to Pit City, knees pressed up against mine in the personal cab, spacious enough for lord and master except when he's got his baby girl's five killers stuffed in there with him.

Side of the Pit. He waits. He paces. I remember the moonlight shone off his hair, silver hair, and thinking how most people didn't age anymore, I mean, given the option, who does? But this guy, let himself get into his fifties before he called a halt to it. It made him mature, and wise. And listened to. Respected. Still young enough, buff, cared for, manicured, but old enough to be senior partner pretty much anywhere he decided to go. Standing here at the Pit in the moonlight with tears on his cheeks waiting for us to do the right thing. Pit full of flames that night, general clean up wash down, we paid our fee and entered; they don't care how you go if you decide to go. And none of us were going. Unblinded. Ungagged. There are workers around the Pit. You can't go around throwing people in just because you want to. It has to be voluntary. And him standin' there waitin' for us to be voluntary and none of us is going. Until Cassie made a move. Hit the big guy himself running and almost toppled him in, worst choice she could've made and when the guns in his goons' hands went off it was my Sal they hit.

I surface again. The holding cell. Where they took us after C ran. Long night of torture. Don't know what the holding cell was initially for– manufacturing plant? Or some kind of water tank? But they're impregnable (too bad Shana wasn't). Long night of screaming because just because we weren't going to HK over this little incident and just because daddy dearest couldn't force us to didn't mean he was going to let us walk away clean. And that's when Cassie ran.

The cab touches down on the crumbling concrete inside the HC. I half expect I'm going to see Sal's crumpled body still there but it was over three years ago and the Undergrounders have taken it, took it probably before we cleared that part of the City. I grind my teeth. Don't know why she came here. Don't know if she knows I'm followin'. Don't know what Tish and George think I'm going to do. After runnin' into her at the Pit yesterday I knew I'd find her again. Cassie. We have a lot to talk about. Looks like it's going to be a long night. We'll let morning decide which of us goes back to the Pit.

*Welcome to the Pit. My name is Manny. How can I help you?*

Saw 'em come in together. Well, not together. They all came in like they were separate, one an' one an' two, but after you've worked here awhile you can tell. Tall girl first, looks like she has a lot on her mind, and not sure she knows she's with the other three. She paid for a soak, not Pit side, so got her deposit and let her in to the baths. And the next girl, little thing, big gray blue eyes, signs her name Sarah and she looks old fashioned like a Sarah, she pretends not to but she takes a look at where Cassie signed in afore her and signs the same and the two after her, I practically have their tickets out an' ready afore they ask. They're together, god bless 'em, got a story t' work through. Not sure my part in the ramblin' will ever be told but I give 'em suits and I give 'em towels and I give 'em all the privacy talk and take their deposits 'case they decide to go ringside. They're together anyway and they've got a lot to talk about and a long night to get through. See a lot of it in the ritual baths.

Lot of untold stories, gettin' told.

*My homage to Mary Poppins, which is both a beloved book and a beloved movie. The first lines always get Bruce Springsteen's "You Can Look (But You Better Not Touch)" from The River stuck in my head. It may actually be where the story started but it went on, at least to my way of thinking, to touch on the theme of loneliness.*
*Bernard Aaronson wrote, "While we are each totally alone, it is an error to confuse this with being lonely."*
*That doesn't mean we're not all looking for someone.*

## Until the Wind Changes

"Sold! To the young man with the wandering hands!" the owner said, clapping Billy on the back and startling the breath out of him.

*No.* He hadn't meant, to, really, he was just looking. Except sometimes his hands did his looking for him, his mother always said.

But there was no way she could afford this, <u>no way</u>. They'd had pasta six times last week, every time with some kind of explanation but he'd seen that look on her face every time the email popped up and she waited to see if it was his father or another creditor, and she had that look again now.

Weren't things bad enough? The whole day at school Daav had been at him, never anything he could actually turn him in for, just mean, and then he'd flunked another math test and that just *had* to pull out because Fleet wouldn't take someone who couldn't handle maths....

The store rushed in on him, all dusty and mote-strewn, advertising finds from the 1990s, the 10s and 20s, but mostly it was junk, piled too close together, slipping and sliding on the tables, piled up under them, and badly in need of dusting. A pile of books, care worn and archaic, and past that, a series of digital books, a left over from the early 00s, and there in their middle, like a siren call to a twelve year old boy, a servant droid, her arms held out in front of her as if her last action had never been completed, her eyes empty and fixed, dusty and staring off toward the window at the other end of the shop, like there was somewhere she had to go if she could just get herself to move again.

And now there was a crack radiating up her left arm from wrist joint to elbow bend, where Billy had looked with his hands and hers had dropped suddenly, sailed down from her hopeful arms-out pose to bump against a smaller, compact trash droid, and the crack had radiated up the alloy until it reached her elbow.

Billy looked away from the droid, away from Mr. Trazini, the owner, and up at his mother, expecting anger, but Marla looked resigned, was just motioning for him to come and stand beside her while she finished up a last few things with the owner, signed her Right To Work papers, maybe, if she'd gotten the job, and what good would that do now?

Stupid, Billy thought. I'm stupid and clumsy and dumb. Daav is right. I'm a genetic error. He toed the carpet of the shop, stared at his feet, and the droid's good right hand brushed against his shoulder, only settling, but it felt as if she'd reached out to pat him.

"Oh, well," Marla said while they waited for the all clear to lift the skiff into the flowing lanes of traffic that blanketed the skies. The afternoon was gray and wet, typical February, with a light ash falling from the factories. Marla was trying to smile, but her eyes were fixed on the droid in the back seat of the skiff, her features blank but her eyes dusted and a light oil applied to her joints, smelling citrusy in the over-warm vehicle. "Maybe she can help out with the housework." She was trying to smile, the way she did so often now that dad was gone. "I could use the help around the house. And maybe she can be company for you two boys." But she had that look on her face again, that expectant email look.

Billy looked away from his mother, out the window of the skiff, and wished things were different.

Sam wasn't there when they got home. At 17, he was no longer expected to check in with Marla for everything he did or every place he went; he just com'd home to let them know if he'd be late for dinner, or not coming at all. Or at least he thought he was old enough for all that and Marla hadn't been arguing with him much in the fourteen months since dad had gone. Sam had gotten a part time job, over Marla's objections, to help out with the bills, and Billy knew she hated it, but he saw her face when the bills queued up on the terminal and he saw her face when Sam came home with his pay check and so things were staying that way for now.

Billy shoved the droid ahead of him into the cramped, dismal kitchen. His mother had hung the curtains from their old house in the windows, routinely bought flowers from the corner store with credits she saved by doing the laundry in the sink and hanging it to dry, but the kitchen remained dark and featureless, chrome surfaces and only about a third of the appliances they'd had before dad--

"Mr. Trazini is going to let me pay it off over my first year," Marla said, coming around to where Billy had stopped with the droid. "He says once we get her charged up and going, we'll have a good little helper." She was staring quizzically into the droid's face before she turned away at a soft chime and crossed the kitchen to que up the terminal.

"Does it hurt?" Billy asked the droid, pointing at the starred and cracking left arm.

"Billy, it's not voice actual--" Marla said from the terminal.

"No," the droid said, in a voice that sounded smooth and human, not the usual shaky and uninflected coldness of computer generated droid speech. "I have no pain sensors." She was looking at Billy and as he looked away from her arm and up to her face, she winked. "It is merely inconvenient."

Billy gaped, staring at the droid, and across the room his mother said, "Well," and then again, an instant later, "Well."

Sam blew in a little after nine that night. Billy was sitting on the edge of his bed, facing Sam's, their twin beds set close together with only the bed stand and single, old-fashioned lamp between them.

"Whatcha doing, squirt?" Sam asked, the way he always did and the way Billy hated. Five years wasn't that long a time between them. It was just forever. It meant Sam was tall and golden and broad shouldered and would be eligible for Fleet in another year while Billy was short, squat, pimply and at the mercy of the Daav's of the world.

Sam bounced on the bed across from him.

"Trig," Billy said, closing the book. It wasn't doing any good anyway. "I'm never going to get it."

"Sure you will. You're only twelve. Give it time."

Time. He didn't have time. "But what about Fleet--" he started and Sam was up again, ruffling his hair, heading for the bathroom.

"You worry too much, squirt. Fleet's a ways off. Don't worry so much." Water started running in the sink across the hall. "Hey, heard you had a run in with a droid today," Sam called back and Billy winced.

"Yeah."

Sam's head popped back around the corner. "Don't take it so hard. Mom's needed help around here forever. T's probably bustin' her for the price, but it's not such a big thing." He withdrew his head and shut the door and Billy sat on the edge of his bed, staring at Sam's, and thinking "It's not such a big thing," but he didn't really believe it.


His eye hurt like hell and he wanted Marla to be home and at the same time he hoped she wouldn't be as he approached the apartment on foot because Daav had taken his skiff pass again. When he shoved the door open she wasn't home but something in the kitchen smelled good and Billy followed the scent to the source.

"What happened to your eye?" Lila asked, sliding across the floor on silent trax. Since she'd been charged and lubed, she'd pretty much taken over running the house and Billy was seeing less of that exhausted look on his mother's face at the end of the day. And he didn't have to worry so much about where he'd dropped his books when he got home, or whether or not he put away his dirty clothes. But he found he kept doing so anyway. He liked Lila, and he liked being around her, and if she was busy cleaning up after him, she didn't have time to sit with him.

"Daav happened to my eye," Billy said, heading for the refrigerator. Milk would probably go best with what was smelling a whole lot like the apple pie Marla used to make before dad went away. Lila beat him to the door.

"Let's take care of that first, shall we?" she asked, taking his hand in hers, the one that ended the cracked and starred plastic arm. She led him over to the sink and wet a clean dishtowel, told him to hold it against his eye where the swelling was starting.

"Does it hurt much?" Lila asked. Her voice still didn't sound like a servo. It was smooth and easy, with no stutterings between words, and it was deep.

"Nah. No pain sensors," Billy said and Lila looked startled, her alloy face taking on a quizzical expression just before she laughed.

"We won't tell your mother about this, shall we? I think she has enough on her mind," Lila said. She pressed the towel a little harder, wrapped Billy's hand over it, and skated over to the sink to cut a wedge of good golden apple pie, juices flowing onto the plate and mingling with the chunk of yellow cheese there.

And for a little while Daav and the other kids at school disappeared while Billy ate and Lila listened to his day.

"Maybe she can help you with your maths," Marla said, because at thirteen, they still weren't coming easily for him.

"But Sam always does that," Billy said fast, too fast, but suddenly it seemed dangerous to let Lila take over that function.

Marla sighed, rising to stand by the window in their latest

apartment, arching her back and soaking up the heat from the early May sunshine. "Sam's not going to be here forever, Billy," she said, and left the living room without looking at him again.

Billy's heart began to pound against his ribs.


"But we always *said*--" He was perched on the edge of his bed, barely sitting, facing Sam whose legs jutted off the too-small twin bed, nearly touching Billy's. It was the first time he'd seen Sam in their room in a long time.

Their room.

Now Billy's.

"I know, Billy-boy. But don't you see? If I wait for you, I'll be five years behind all the other guys my age." He looked hopefully at Billy, like maybe he wouldn't see the crystalline tears puddling in the corners of Billy's eyes and creeping down the sides of his face. "You'll catch up, squirt. I'll still be there when you get there."

But he wouldn't, really. This was Sam. He'd be an officer by then, no doubt, or running the whole damn Fleet. He wouldn't be hanging out waiting for his little brother to arrive, he'd be off with his friends, saving the universe.

"I'm sorry, squirt," Sam said, reaching over to ruffle his hair the way Billy hated. "You get it, don't you?"

Billy shrugged, not looking up, still perched on the edge of the bed, his head in his hands, and after a while Sam left the bedroom and after a while longer, Lila rolled in, her weight on the bed tipping Billy easily into her embrace.


"For the love of Saturn, you're fifteen years old," Marla said impatiently. She needed to get going, drop Billy at school, open the store for Eric T. "Why can't you just respond to Daav the same way he treats you?"

Billy hung his head, wishing Sam were there. "You don't understand," he said miserably. "Please, mom, just today. Let me stay home today." He knew he had that look on his face again, hang dog, the way Marla had before she became a partner in the store and stopped looking so terrified every time the email blipped.

"Fine," she said abruptly, moving toward the door. "I don't have time for this. Get Lila to walk you through your maths, then. I don't want you spending the whole day on the vids." And she was gone, having only got home just as he woke up, and he didn't have the heart to ask if she'd been with Trazini.

Soft tread on the carpet but he didn't look around.

"It's good for her," Lila said. "She needs this involvement. You're growing up so fast, you won't be here for her much longer." Her eyes softened as she looked at him, her arms out as if she wanted to hold him.

"I'm not here for her right now," Billy said flatly. "Not that she knows, anyway." He rested his head against her shoulder as she stroked his hair and her shoulder felt softer than plastic, warmer than servo.

"Now, why don't we discuss what would happen if you just *ignored* Daav altogether."

Billy pulled back to look into her face. "That's what you always tell me to do," he protested.

Lila looked unrepentant. "Have you ever tried it?" She waited.

"--No."

"Well, then, Lila said and sounded very like his mother had used to.

"I don't understand why you're not going to the dance," Marla said. She wasn't looking at him, was making that frozen rabbit face she always made when she applied lipstick, pulling her upper lip down until he thought her nose would wiggle and then pushing both lips out like a duck bill. "It's Zero G. I thought you liked that."

He did, or at least he had, back when he thought he still had a shot at Fleet. But with his grades, that was looking more and more unlikely. Billy shrugged. Marla caught the move in the mirror, frowned slightly as she started the next coat of greenish tinged paint. "I saw Ariel's mother in the store today. She said Ariel's going to be there." A slight, very calculated pause. "I thought you and Ariel--" She let the question trail off, concentrated on her eye lashes.

"She's going with Daav," Billy said, and left the bathroom.

Marla followed him. "You need to go out. You've got to meet people. You don't have any friends!" She was picking up her wrap, which was changing colors as fast as it could to compensate for the wild swirls of her party dress. She tucked her hair back up into the latest do, a sort of wild sticky affair that looked like a bird's nest after a bad storm. "Come on, Billy, I'll drop you at the party on my way. You shouldn't be home alone so much." Her eyes were mothering, imploring, but impatience was half an instant from checking the LED embedded in her wrist.

"I'm not going," Billy said. "I'm going to stay home and work on my maths."

Marla sighed. "You really do need friends," she said, already starting for the door.

"Lila's my friend."

"Billy, she's *artificial intelligence*," Marla said, sounding exasperated. She held the door open with one hand against it as if still expecting Billy to go through it, but after thirty seconds she sighed and went through it alone.

"No, she's not," Billy said softly to the closed door. She was a lot more real than some people.

"You should have gone to the dance," Lila said. She was cleaning off the kitchen counter tops, servos whining softly. Billy relaxed with the sound. For him it meant home, it meant no Daavs and no checking terminal for e's from Sam, who almost never wrote now that he was actually assigned out and somewhere across the world on a peace keeping tour. The sound of Lila, smoothly, effortlessly moving about the kitchen made Billy's shoulders drop from their protective height.

"Why?"

Lila looked at him for an instant before lowering a handful of dishes into the soapsuds. "Because it would have been good for you. Because you have to go out there eventually. Because you're headed for Fleet and should have fun while you can."

"I'll never make Fleet," Billy said. "My maths are nowhere near good enough."

Lila shrugged. "Because you're sixteen years old and you should be out with your friends, not here with me."

"You're my friend," Billy said, feeling mutinous.

"Yes, I am," Lila said, and sighed, a lot like Marla did.

They sent Sam's body home in a little box, already cremated and sealed in a faux granite stone, the way they always did now that peace keeping had become war maintenance. The stone would sit nicely on a shelf, holding up a line of digitals or keeping Marla's flowers from tipping over too far when she forgot to replace them and they started to sag.

"What do I do now?" Billy asked, slumped across his bed and staring at the one that had once been Sam's. He hadn't occupied it in three years, but it was still his, unchanged, unchanging, the way Sam was now.

"What you and Sam were going to do," Lila said, folding his shirts, tucking them away in the drawer before she slid it back into the featureless, pale wall. "What you had planned. What Sam wanted you to do."

She stood with her arms folded, looking down at him, loving and stern and not able to let this tragedy derail her boy. "What you're so very capable of doing."

"My maths--"

"Are an excuse," Lila said, and her voice rose, sharp, the way it sometimes did, the way servos shouldn't manage to do. "You know it and I know it. Maths aren't the number one thing. Look at your languages. How many do you speak? You can 'face with computers, Bill. You can speak five languages."

"Six," Billy said.

"Six." She stood waiting but he wasn't inclined to say anymore, so she did. "There's science, and language, and the physical, and you'll pass them all. You've grown five feet in the last five minutes," she said but he didn't smile, didn't even look up. "You'll make it, Bill. Just have a little faith in yourself."

"No one else does," Billy flared, looking up just in time to see the spark of disappointment in the eyes that would never be able to register emotion.

"You're so wrong," Lila said softly and rolled her way to

the door, where she turned and said again, "You're so very wrong."

"She's beautiful," he said, grinning at Lila over the top of his glass. He couldn't remember the last time he'd sat at the kitchen table after school and let her feed him a snack. Lately it was all training, all preparing for Fleet tryouts, all looking toward the future and already home was falling away into the past. "Most girls at school, you know, they're cute. But she's beautiful." He swallowed and took another bite. Lila's apple pie still knew no equal. "Daav asked her to the dance but you know what? She turned him down. I think she likes me." He blushed even as he said it and Lila stood, taking his glass and plate, moving toward the sink with them. Her trax seemed a little louder, her movements a little slower. Billy blinked and everything seemed normal again.

"Are you going to ask her?" Lila asked without turning around and Billy paused, as if considering when he actually already knew the answer. Then,

"Yeah. Yeah, I think I am," Billy said and he watched Lila lower the dishes into the sink and thought she was probably smiling.

"Billy, it's just the wrong day," Marla's voice said over the com. He'd left the view screen off, was just listening to her voice, because he didn't want to know where she was calling from.

"It's grad, mom," Billy said. "They don't schedule it around *your* schedule.'

"Don't be impertinent," Marla said and Billy sighed. Her voice came again, lower, wheedling.

"Billy, please. This is such a chance. Mr. T. and I have a

once in a lifetime opportunity to auction, to really get our hands on some prizes from the twentieth century. I'm sorry I'm going to miss grad, honey, but--"

"It's OK," Billy said, abruptly readying to term com. "I'll ask Lila to go."

"Oh, that's a--" but he hit disconnect and her last words were lost in the static and his own thoughts.

When he found Lila she was in the utility room, running a program through the computer that would clean some of the fallout out of the air. He noticed she was moving slowly and that her fingers on the keys sounded like sharp, hard plastic tapping away. When he touched her shoulder she turned sluggishly and he realized her eyes were dusty and that she wasn't blinking.

I need to spend more time with her, he thought, but he was already on his way out the door and it would have to be later.


Fleet tryouts were the week after grad, when Lila had taken him for a very late dinner after he got home. He'd seen her in the audience, her face as proud and beaming as his mother's absent face should have been, but he got turned around in the crush of students and hadn't seen her again until late that night, after party, and that's when they'd gone out to get something to eat.

His stomach felt like steel springs were uncoiling in it.

Lila was cleaning the living room, unfailing, unceasing, moving gently along the rug cleaning stray bits of ash and using her censors to monitor the air. He hadn't seen her do that in a long time and the array of lights across her wrists and chest panel seemed alien and inhuman. But the news overshadowed and as soon as he stood her eyes cleared and she let the lights dim until they matched the rest of her alloy.

"Accepted for Fleet tryouts," he crowed and she reached out for him, gave him a quick hard hug in keeping with his excitement, let him bound away from her and come back on his own, the way he always had. The way she always had.

"You'll come?" he asked, almost a demand. Of course she would. She always did. She always had.

Lila shook her head. "No." Before he could speak, she said it again. "No. No, Bill, not this time. This time you need to do it alone." Her arms were folded, the left over the right, the shattered place showing under the sleeve of her house dress.

"But I can't," he all but wailed. Counting on her. She had to be there. She was always there.

Lila shook her head again. "But you come home afterward, tell me about it. I'll be here," she said, but there was an undercurrent of doubt in her voice as she turned and rolled away, somewhat jerking, uncoordinated. Her trax caught the corner of the wall and it threw her a little off balance as she went. At the last second, she turned and smiled at him, and said, "You'll make it, Billy. I've always know that. You're there, now." And before he could say anything, ask anything, demand anything at all, Lila said, "Goodbye," and rolled out of sight.

It was late when he got home, and dark, and there was no sign of Marla's skiff in the dock. He was still a little tipsy and Emerald's last kiss was still warming his lips when he swung the front door open and saw the banners she'd hung up.

"Congratulations," the letters spelled out, only she'd got the U and the L mixed up so it read "congrat-lua-tions" and it made Billy laugh, standing there with the windy spring night behind him and the future ahead. The tryouts had been a piece of cake. He was bigger now than Sam had ever been and Lila had been right, maths hadn't weighed in for much at all.

"Lila?"

Abruptly aware there was too much silence in the house.

"Lila?"

She wasn't in the kitchen, although there was a cake on the table, his name spelled out but kind of falling away at the end.

"Lila?" His voice softer now. There was a light burning in the utility room, but it looked wrong, more like a console read out light. He squinted against it, his head aching a little, padded through the arch and into the utility room.

She was rolling back and forth, doing the laundry, doing the windows, efficient, ceaseless, trusty, her joints clicking a little from the cold, her treads whining as they hissed over the tile.

"Lila?" Very quiet now.

She turned and looked at him, flat eyes, needing dusting. The crack in her arm. The shapeless dress, that hung like a furniture cover. "Yes."

He swallowed. "I did it. I got it. I passed Fleet tests. I'm in." Tried to sound enthusiastic. Tried to project life into his words, into hers. Waited while her servos clicked and whined. A pause, then,

"Con-grat-u-la-tions," she said in a mechanical voice, only a little colder and more lifeless than the room around her. Billy swallowed again and Lila turned back to the laundry, unaware of his presence, simply moving about her tasks.

Con-grat-u-la-tions. Congrat-lua-tions.

He went back to the kitchen where the cake sat on the

table, his name running away at the end so it read Billll, rather than Billy, and he sat at the table and thought about the future and about the past and about the costs of growing up.

"Mommy, she winked at me," the little girl said. "The plastic lady winked at me."

"Hush, Jill," her mother said, one hand absently patting. "Mommy's in a hurry. The lady is an android, dear, and droids don't wink at people." She looked up as the clerk came toward her, a middle aged woman whose name tag read Marla, who wove her way through the maze of archaic offerings gathering dust in the dim light of the antique shop.

Jill moved away from her mother, her hands carefully behind her back the way she'd been taught wherever they went anywhere. She stood on her tip toes and stared up into the plastic lady's eyes, started hard, wanting to see, and an instant later the droid blinked. Jill gave a little cry, bounced back in surprise, and one of the droid's arms suddenly swung down, a sharp clack as it connected with the table beside it and then her mother and Miss Marla, the shop's owner, were there, and her mother was saying, "I'm so sorry, she usually doesn't," and Miss Marla was saying, "Yes, but I'm afraid it's the store's policy, if you break it, you've bought it. Yes, I know, if I could just have your purchase chit-- thank you," and then, "once you get her cleaned up and charged, you'll have a wonderful housekeeper. I had this one for years and my son just loved her."

They moved toward the terminal and their voices faded away as Jill leaned closer to the droid, looking up from the crack along the arm, up again into her eyes. The plastic lady smiled and it didn't look at all like a machine, not like

Mommy had always told her droids were.

The plastic lady winked again and this time when Jill winked back she said, "My name is Lila. What's yours?"

*I can no longer remember what the anthology was where the call for submissions made me start researching the Comfort Women, a controversial term for girls and women kidnapped and forced into prostitution during World War II.*
*I'd never heard of this, and my research was horrifying and short-lived and the story, whatever it was, never got written.*
*Some time later the research I'd done bobbed up in my head again, this time crossed with a nonfiction story I'd done on mining, most likely, and speculation about what humans might do to other planets once we have the ability to go and "harvest" whatever we want wherever we want. All the ideas came together to create a brutal story that sold to J. Alex Erwine at The 5th Di...*

## Cold Comfort

Light from a number of moons lit the powdered ice, making the ground a glittering mirror of the ink black lightless spill of stars overhead. Mae had looked up twice when she came here and each time her captors had clubbed her back down for daring to raise her head. She had not looked up since. Now her world was eye level and below. She knew the insignia of Earth Korps and the Kahn Warriors and they were supposed to be enemies but EK came here a lot. NASU, North American States United, decried war crimes and their soldiers participated in them.

The soldier gripping her arm from behind and steering her harshly was Kahn Warrior, enormous, Chinese, a huge moustache covering his lower face and his cheese colored skin pock marked from some childhood illness. Unlike some of the soldiers who simply dragged the girls wherever they were wanted, this one was awake. His eyes glittered, alert and aware and filled with some undirected anger, some bright need to hurt.

He wore fur and leather boots and a heavy jacket with the hood covering his long black hair.

Mae wore a short sleeved shift that could be ripped away at a moment's notice and sandals with socks because some men cared about the girls' feet and so frostbite had to be prevented.

The fist wrapped around her upper arm jerked hard and Mae floundered on the cutting ice, afraid she was going to fall. Light poured out of the sex barracks where she assumed she was being led. Night after night after night, sweating stinking men against the arctic night, but at least it was warm there. The soldier didn't give her time to recover from her stumble – he dragged her and Mae let herself fall into step rather than trip or run to catch up. One ankle twisted partially, hot pain burning up her outer calf against the dry, hard cold. With the change of direction she let herself look up fractionally, the quickest of glances to gauge the terrain ahead, to see where she was being taken.

The shock that lanced through her was colder than the icy night she moved in. Mae wrenched back against the soldier instinctively, twisting and kicking. The sandals went flying and the ice knifed through the socks. Fists numb, skin hard with cold, she battered him and he laughed, then threw her down in the snow, the cotton shift no protection at all. Mae's breath left in a gasp and her body arced in on itself, no way to get to her feet, no way to run and nowhere to run to on this planet. Death would find her out there if it didn't find her right here and she tried to curl around herself, waiting for the inevitable boot to connect with her hips, her belly, her spine. But the soldier just snarled something and dragged her up again and she was too breathless and too shocked and too horrified to fight again.

The women's screams were too much for some human soldiers. They'd found the sounds distasteful, disturbing. So the military had built one secure, soundproof building where the women could be taken and the soldiers wouldn't be disturbed. Nothing separated the sounds inside. Nothing stopped the girls from hearing each other's suffering. Nothing stopped the screams, except when they suddenly broke off inside the Silent Barracks.

"I can break your neck," the soldier said when she started to fight again, ineffectual but enough to annoy him.

*No, you can't*, she wanted to say. But he could break her arm. Dislocate her shoulder. And no one would do anything until the doctor came, checking for VD, carrying off any dead. Then she might put it back or set it or splint it, if she felt like it. That the doctor was a woman was appalling. But it was not the worst thing on this cold planet where the safest base camps were in the snow zone. The worst things were in the building the soldier was dragging her to.

The warmth clubbed her like a fist. After being in the snow and out in the night, the building seemed violently overheated, stuffy until she thought she couldn't breathe. Inside was unadorned: hallways with tired industrial carpet, walls insulated to dull sound but mostly to keep it from reaching the outdoors. Hallways, hung with pictures of women, pornographic, rank, hedonistic, vile. Homicidal. Mae went limp. No point fighting, she'd only get herself hurt before she needed to. Once inside the grey metal fortress the doors locked automatically. From the inside the only way out was with a key. From the outside the doors were completely unlocked – no one chose to come in here.

Into the warren of hallways, brutal metal doors with small glass and mesh windows. Lights over the doors, color-coded. Green meant available. Yellow meant someone waited for a girl inside. Red was the universal symbol of danger, of stop, of do not proceed at all costs: red meant the room was occupied, that there was a girl inside and that she was not alone. That there was, or soon would be, or recently had been, screaming.

The deep purple light meant clean up was required.

The room was empty but full of the smell of whatever had gone on before. Mae's heart trip hammered from the smell, hot salt, like an ocean, and metallic tang, like blood. Wet wool, the shaggy, terrifying scent of the beings. Atavistic response made her spin and pound aching hard fists against the metal core door. There was no point, just as there was no way not to try.

The door held. She exhausted herself against it, skinned the edges of her hands, lost her balance and hit her head, screamed till she was hoarse as if there was anyone who could help her. There were only prisoners and guards here. There was no one to care. No one was going to help.

At last she slid down the door, her back against it, her long black hair fanning up it as she fell, then showering around her head and shoulders. Her breath came irregularly in hitches of fear. Last time she had been brought here had been a thousand times worse than anything any of the soldiers had ever done to her. Last time the creature had touched her in ways that made her nerves scream as if she was being electrified. He – it – had found all her joints, all the places nerves were high, had touched them all like a burning brand till she was too exhausted to move, until she could barely make a sound. Only then had it taken her, used her as aid-and-comfort workers were intended to be used. Her contribution to the war effort.

A war that wasn't hers on a planet that wasn't home.

In Korea, in Namp'o, the cherry trees would be past their bloom. The green season would be upon the land, summer sweltering inland from the coast, everything green and lush and hotter even than this prison room with its bed and chains and lights over the doors for clean up when the indigenous beings went too far. The beings who controlled the minerals Earth Forces fought over with each other. With other beings from other worlds. Once Earth had seen value here, factions had come and then soldiers had come and then sex workers had come and, because of that, VD had come. And Earth governments, in their glory, had sent aid-and-comfort women to Altarus.

No one volunteered. So volunteers were recruited.

She was 23 and 3/4. She wanted very much to see 24.

On Earth. Back in Korea.

Her heart pounded pitifully, a thin thudding defense against the terror that would come through those doors.

With her eyes closed, she could still see the dock in the willows where Li used to bring the boat, where they'd spend long hours lying together, cramped and uncaring, staring up at the summer sky and imagining their future together.

If she tried, she could remember her mother's face when she'd smile and hold her arms out to welcome Mae back from school or home from dates.

Her eyes opened. Li was dead. And after she'd been used such, her mother could never possibly open her arms to Mae again. If she could get back to Earth, if she could survive the war in this brutal place, it would all be for nothing anyway.

Across form her, the door opened. The creature entered the room like a small earthquake. Too enormous for Mae to accept at first, as if he went on past the boundaries of her vision. The smell was instant and overwhelming, shaggy and cloying like wet animals, a smell that got inside and woke a girl a week or a month later, a smell as real and immediate as the nightmare relivings of the rapes.

It was so much bigger than her. She could run past it, through the opened door, the way an irresponsible dog runs between the legs of a human owner in a bid for freedom.

There was no freedom. The only things on the other side of the far door were guards and soldiers and monsters and the killing cold of the frost giant everyone was marooned on for the duration of the hostilities. Other girls had tried it, overcome with terror. Other girls had died.

There were so many ways to die here. There was no point in pushing it.

Mae lifted her head and shoved herself back against the door, sitting upright. The smell of the creature brought back the pain from the previous month, how many Earth-weeks ago? She'd healed but everything felt fragile. Her body was brittle now, twig-dry with the cold, hard with terror; easily broken.

She did not want to be broken again. She didn't want to

die.

But she was tired of never looking up. She was tired of being beaten and lost.

There were so many ways to get hurt here. Sometimes that fact afforded a tiny freedom.

Mae looked up at the creature across from her and locked her gaze with its.

The eyes were golden brown and intelligent. When it saw her looking it lowered its massive head as if trying to look less threatening and then, abruptly, it shoved the door closed behind it and put its back against the door and slowly slid down until it sat, facing Mae across the tiny room.

*What are you waiting for?* But waiting was no worse torture than being touched. Or maybe it was. The anticipation of the pain. Of the violation that would come afterwards.

When she met its eyes again she saw no promise of pain in them, but when it reached a hand out toward her Mae scrabbled up the door onto her feet and tried to back away. The being instantly dropped its hands again. "How long since slept?"

"– what?" She'd known they could speak, though human speech seemed to hurt them. The question confused her. She made no movement but watched the being the way a mouse would watch a cat that hadn't tried to eat it yet.

The creature stirred. "Must be hard. To sleep. Here. So many others." It gestured and Mae felt laughter straining, inappropriate and maybe deadly. It meant the other girls. "And so many." It paused and thought and finished, "Men."

Certainly made sense to pause before men. Men Mae had known didn't hurt and rape and kill. But her questioner waited for an answer and Mae said tentatively, "If you sleep too much – you wake up to bad things?" Would he understand her?

The shaggy head nodded. Abruptly he fell into speech, fast as if determined to finish speaking before the pain grew too great. "Your people honor me here. To refuse would dishonor my people. My people kill for such things."

"Kill?" It was the second thing she'd said. "You? Or me?"

The being shrugged, a rippling of dark hair. "Or you. Both. I have hours," he said and she realized he meant in the room. "You could sleep."

Mae stared and when the creature gestured at the bed she could not stop herself from looking. It seemed a generosity too big to be considered, a luxury too wonderful to believe. A bed with blankets and a pillow. To sleep, to really sleep, and to wake without being beaten out of sleep by guards angry she wasn't awake and attentive, to not wake in the midst of yet another rape, of the other girls by rank and file men who didn't warrant a compliance room. Or to wake in the process of her own rape.

Even if it were a lie. Even if it were only for a few minutes. How wonderful to sleep.

She kept her eyes on the creature as she moved toward the bed but he never moved, only followed her with his eyes.

The bed felt like heaven, the pillow smooth under her cheek. Despite the heat in the room she pulled the covers up, grateful to have them around her. She risked a glance at the creature, ready to find this had been a trap or a lie. But he had settled himself more comfortably against the door, head tipped back and eyes closed. She thought he was asleep. Mae closed her eyes, nestled into the pocket of warmth she had made, and slept.

She woke slowly. With her eyes still closed and the warmth of the bed around her, disorientation thrummed through her. There was no sense of panic, only of gentle confusion and warmth. Someone stroked her hair, slowly and softly, a hand running from the crown of her head down over the back of her neck and shoulders. Gentle, rhythmic, slow. She swam up through layers of sleep, imagining she was young, a child still, maybe waking from a long illness. Or that she lay with Li, some slow interlude, perhaps she'd fallen asleep watching a movie, waking slowly in the dark with Li touching her.

But Li was dead. Even in a half sleep she could never not know that.

When she opened her eyes the sound-proofed room rose up around her and the gentle stroking stopped. She stayed still, waiting, pensive as an animal scenting for danger, but nothing happened.

She turned toward the creature in the room who had so recently let off touching her and he rose soundlessly and retreated, as far from her as he could get.

Mae sat up slowly, letting the covers fall away. The room was still brutally hot. The cotton shift had twisted around her as she slept but she still wore it. She looked away from her toes against the industrial carpet and up at the being in the room with her.

"Are you going to hurt me?" she asked finally. There were no clocks in the room but it felt like she had slept for several hours. Now awake the fear was returning. The fear, and the anticipation of it.

He shook his head at hers, his eyes not leaving hers. One down.

"Are you going to rape me?"

He looked contemplative for a moment before he shook his head again. "They honor me with you." He didn't look away from her. "They do not need to know to what extent I appreciate their honor."

That made her laugh. Foolish or not, she relaxed then, and her muscles unknotted.

There came the sudden sound of footsteps in the hall and suddenly she knew she'd squandered this time. There were questions she should have asked. Who he was and why he was different. Why he hadn't hurt her when the last monster had. Their race. Their customs. If he would help her.

He couldn't. Of course. His people honored him with a whore. They'd execute him if he refused the honor. It didn't sound like a race that would allow him any leeway to help her.

Knowledge, then. Some kind of understanding. Was there a way the girls could avoid being hurt by the others? Some thing they could do, some need they could meet without pain and sometimes death? But the footsteps were at the door. She'd hear the knock in an instant, five minute warning for the male. That knock that made everything so much worse every other time when five minutes had expanded to encompass the universe and all of time.

Now–

"What do you – I mean, your people, why –"

The knock sounded, five quick taps. But instead of acknowledging the creature turned and opened the door as if it had never been locked. He turned back to her and met her gaze, standing in the doorway with a Kahn Warrior behind him, and said simply, "I'm sorry."

Winter thickened. The bleak horizon disappeared into

greyouts, frozen ice crystals creating cutting blizzards with gale-force winds. The planet's atmosphere was thin, the nights dark, the days – when the ice cloud cover lifted – blinding. The cold grew intense and the guards grew restless and angry, shoving the girls into crouch boxes or out into the snow for hours at the slightest provocation. Supplies grew thin and would remain so until the optimistically named spring allowed supply ships in more plentifully. Talk of the war escalated, or even the war itself. A casual brutality increased. Men who had been content to rape, to take what wasn't theirs, to maybe call a girl by a remembered lover's name now raged and fought. Girls were thrown down and brutalized; faces buried in pillows, breath too short. Hair was wrapped over faces and around throats. Fists were used where hands would have sufficed – few of the girls had much fight left in them. There was too much fear and they were too hungry, reduced to stealing scraps from the food they prepared for the soldiers while the storms grew worse and worse.

Everyone worked harder, just to survive, except the girls, who worked harder so everyone else could survive. Three of the girls died, too hungry and too tired to survive their cruelest lovers. New girls were brought in when the storms lifted enough. A shipment of meat and already-tired produce came in, along with four new girls too terrified and beaten and despondent to be much more than a liability for the seasoned girls who were supposed to watch over and teach them. Mae got assigned to the laundry, where there was no chance to steal food, and her days fell into a grey twilight of hunger and exhaustion, her nights into a hell of rape and abuse and fear. And waiting. Because something had to change. And she thought, even if it was impossible, that something had already started to change.

Something was changing inside her.

She started to dream. Dreaming wasn't welcome here. Memories hurt. Remembering realities that would never come again was painful. And most dreams were nightmares.

Hers were, long, damaging dreams of rape and rapists, of pain and suffering, of Li and loss and everything she would never have again crossed with the times in the crouch boxes mixed with the times in the Silent Barracks. All nightmares.

And then, unexpectedly, the dreams changed. As if they weren't hers, they led her through stories she didn't know. The dreams showed her places she'd never been. And there was no pain in them, no suffering, no fear.

But they were on Altarus. In the war. They were dreams of ice storms and kitchen brawls and the tankers that brought supplies but there was more in them Mae seemed outside herself, a visitor, an observer. She watched her own self the way she'd once watched movies she didn't particularly care about and after a while she saw the dreams were leading somewhere.

"Pay attention," Sukie said and all but slapped Mae with a handful of wet linens. Steam from the wash tub eddied up around them but it chilled in the air before it could warm them. The air in the laundry was wet and cold, like the ocean shore in winter in Korea, only smelling of bleach.

The bleach could never completely fade the blood stains.

More indigenous creatures were brought in now, wide eyed shambling monsters with hideous appetites and a desire for pain. They watched the girls and they worked with the Kahn Warriors and the American military and the indigenous troops and eventually they did something to warrant praise and reward and then they'd ask for a girl. They'd walk the line up, looking at faces, looking into eyes to find the girls who would scream the loudest and ache the most. Two of the new girls died within days of their arrival. Mae thought them lucky. Twice Kahn Warriors came to her and dragged her screaming through the cutting powdered ice into the Silent Barracks. Once she was forced to wait, kneeling on the filthy hard industrial carpet outside a room while the purple light glared and inside the room a clean up team worked. She saw dripping red sheets pulled out, and after the room was clean but still reeked of blood and fear and pain, Mae was dragged inside, her heart beating too hard and fast, unable to breathe, unable to think. All she could do was scream as the creature came toward her still covered in blood, hands reaching and face leering. In the end it was only the burning touch of the creature. In the end it was only rape, brutal and total but she was alive. She was relatively unhurt.

She never saw Sukie again.

As the warrior dragged her, her own blood on her legs and staining the snow, she saw the creature that had let her sleep, the one with the bright spot in his eye.

The one who had started the change the night's events had set into motion. Mae raised her hand. A greeting. She raised her head without thinking. She met the creature's eyes for an instant before the guard brought his fist down on the back of her neck.

She slumped then, and let him drag her, skin abrading and tearing on the icy snow. It was her night to assist the girls in getting whatever meager dinner they would have together.

Instead, she crawled to her room and tried to breathe

through ribs that ached with every pained breath. She stanched the blood and crawled into bed and tried to stop shaking.

Tried to cry. One of the new girls brought her food. Another who had some medical training but spoke an unknown language treated her wounds. Mae ate and slept and tried to grieve, for everything and everyone lost.

Instead, she dreamed.

She dreamed of ice flows and other places. She dreamed of creatures without fear and without harm. She dreamed of Li but in the dream he was not Li, he was a promise of something. Some future. Some possibility. As if someone had looked into her mind and seen and understood that Li was everything that had ever meant love and joy and happiness. A symbol of Korea, and Earth.

When the harsh grey light of frozen dawn peeled back the dark she woke in pain, her body wracked with chills and sprains and bruises and fever. She rose anyway, assigned to the kitchen. That day where she ate three tomatoes before she could stop herself and no one ever noticed or asked what had happened to them. The food worked wonders on her head. The world became clear and brighter. Around her soldiers moved and creatures shambled and the girls cowered, afraid. Prisoners of war in a sense. Comfort women brought to serve the needs of men, as though to keep them from the ravages of VD and indifferent breeding on this new world. Comfort women, there to ease the soldiers' pain at being so far from home, their own pain doubled and trebled by men who had gone native within weeks of landing on Altarus. As if something there changed them.

There was nothing else on Altarus. This frozen outpost and others like it. That's all humanity had brought to the stars yet. That's what everyone said. There were no cities. There was no help. There was no way out. There was no part of the planet not covered in ice and blood and creatures.

According to the military.

Which was the force that had brought them this incarceration, this torture.

Of course you should always trust the word of the enemy. They're so apt to tell the truth. And the NASU was the enemy.

At some point during the night, which was miraculously long and free of interruptions or screaming or attack, she dreamed that there was help to be found on this world, and that there was somewhere to go. She dreamed the creature told her, the one who hadn't hurt her.

A foolish, suicidal dream. She got up when she was supposed to and went to the kitchen when she was told to and she ate more tomatoes and this time she got noticed but no one did anything about it. So she ate an apple and this time a soldier noticed but he only slapped her and took the rest of it which made Mae think maybe he wasn't rated for fresh food either, so probably he wouldn't report her to anyone higher up the food chain.

She worked in the kitchen through breakfast, lunch and dinner and she ate the scraps the soldiers left and saved some for the remaining new girls. Outside the snow fell, unrelenting, from a battle grey sky. When night fell the change was almost imperceptible.

She started looking forward to sleeping before dinner was served.

Stuck in the kitchen, cleaning and eating and talking with the girls from coastal cities and Korean highlands and the one little lost girl from Okinawa, she missed the evening lineup and by the time she was out of the kitchen there were no men in the lineup room and she slipped away to her bed in the dorm and closed her eyes almost eagerly.

This time she dreamed of the creature itself. He stood somewhere uncertain, grey as the sky and land and snow of this planet and the spot in his one eye blazed. He faced her squarely in the dream, and his words seemed both inside her and without.

*Ask who you would never. Look for help in the place you would think least likely. Run to what you do not believe exists.*

Mae put her hand out to ask him what he meant, what any of it meant, if this was anything but a dream, but rough hands shook her awake, two men shaking her like she was a rag doll between them, not waiting for her to wake completely but taking her between them, hot faces against her neck, rough hands on her breasts, her arms, her back. She kicked and thrashed, taken unaware, tried to scream but they crushed the breath out of her and when she caught it back one of them slugged her hard in the stomach. Dark lights spun behind her eyes. The dream spun away, a fantasy, the kind of thing that could get you killed here. There were so many ways to die on Altarus. The trick was to avoid it.

When she lay still they tired of her and finished their pleasure. One of them slapped her hard as he pulled away. Mae let her head rock across her bed, unresisting, but the other soldier pulled the first off her, shouted something at him and punched him across the jaw. There was a short, hard silence before the one who had slapped her zipped his uniform and left the room.

The other soldier hesitated. Mae lay tense, every muscle hard, waiting for him to leave before the shaking started, before the tears were irreversible. Instead of leaving he came closer to the bed, one calloused hand swept the hair out of her face, gentled it across her forehead and her neck. He dropped something onto the bed beside her head and turned instantly and walked away. When she was sure he was gone she turned her head to see what he had left. A meal chit, which was worth its weight in gold, several of them could eat one meal meant for soldiers. And beside it, script, the money of the world of Altarus.

"*I'm not a whore,*" Mae whispered furiously, afraid to make a sound.

But she kept the money.

The doctor showed up unexpectedly. A flurry of anxiety passed through the girls. The doctor meant more food, sometimes, and right now they were all but starving. She could sometimes give out drugs to make some of the hurt go away and when she was in a really good mood and things were really lucky she gave out drugs to make reality go away. She could treat sprains and cuts and set bones though she didn't always bother and her records were so incomplete that more than one girl had been dosed with Depo-Pronova X enough times so close together to get very sick.

When it came to the doctor, she was simply better than nothing.

Marginally. She didn't bother to close the door during the girl's exams and half the time those comprised the day's entertainment for the men. Even with all the rapes and all the abuse, somehow Mae found that worse. No matter how many times her clothes were stripped from her she never adjusted.

That the doctor was a woman simply made it all the more appalling.

This day the doctor's hands were gentle. Her breath was less ragged and Mae found herself wondering how captive the doctor herself was, whether she hardened herself for a job she didn't dare feel. Today she touched Mae's glands around her neck and listened to her chest as she took deep breaths. Her fingers were cold as she touched Mae's ribs.

"Do you know when these were broken?"

Mae hadn't even known that they were, only that breathing hurt and grated.

She moved slower today and asked questions Mae didn't understand. Was she sleeping? How much food was she getting? Could she get more? How was her strength? Mae, warm in the room, relaxed. The pains of the night fell away. Just having someone touch her without trying to cause harm made her drift inside herself, nearly asleep. And, close to sleep, she thought of the dreams the creature had sent her.

*Ask for help where you would never expect it.*

She didn't expect it, anywhere, here. But things were already so different and strange.

There was nothing to lose. If the doctor reported her she could be beaten or starved or punished in some other way. The way things had been going lately, she had nothing to lose.

"What's out there?" she asked when the doctor, who seemed to be moving ever more slowly, almost as if waiting, paused between her own questions.

Startled, the doctor met Mae's eyes. Hers were deep blue and so tired Mae felt sorry she had asked the question. She thought she'd feel guilty even if the doctor reported her and she was punished.

"Like this," the doctor said. Her eyes flickered briefly around them and back to Mae. There was a small window in the door and while there was no one there, she kept her hands moving, checking for injuries. "For a long distance it's like this. Ice and snow. Barren. But late afternoon right now the sun lights a path through the trees, a place where the trees have been cut."

Inside her angry grating ribs, Mae's heart began to pound.

"If you follow it, if you take the sun line." She stopped. Took a breath. And Mae knew in that moment the doctor had put herself at risk, knew the other woman was truly a prisoner also, and terrified. And determined.

"Take the sun path and walk until sunset. There's – people," she said, and then, "Women."

Mae felt her eyes widen. *Women*, the doctor had said. Not people. Not creatures. A place. Not a city. Just a place.

"But what–"

Hard banging on the door. A Kahn Warrior leered at Mae where she sat on the table, her shift pooled around her hips. She let her features go slack and numb and the doctor called out, loud and angry, "In a minute, you goons really fucked this one up." Which made the face leer again with pleasure and disappear.

"Don't take long," she said the minute the light reappeared and the head in the doorway had vanished.

"Because the light will change," Mae guessed.

"That, too," the doctor said and have her just long enough to get her shift around her before she opened the door, threw Mae out stumbling and barked, "Send in the next whore!"

She didn't tell anyone. Because it couldn't really have happened. The doctor couldn't really have told her something to help her. There couldn't really be somewhere to go on Altarus. It was a dream.

She didn't tell anyone because she didn't want the dream to shatter.

It could easily have been a dream. An hallucination. Mae walked all the time now in a twilight of confusion and hunger, between worlds. It could easily be a dream here, and a path of sunlight seemed the stuff of dreams.

That night there were executions. More and more often it seemed the Kahn Warriors were quarreling amongst themselves, Earth Korps was in shambles and the creatures were cleaning house from inside out. Sharp reports came from outside and the screams of the dying inefficiently dispatched. Two of the girls shook so hard they were useless. Another vomited and couldn't stop. Mae covered for them, moving fast enough in her floating state that they weren't missed. Three of the officers slapped her for being careless and one beat her with his tray when she spilled his coffee. She threw the rest of it in his face when he was done and he dragged her screaming to the Silent Barracks.

"That was *stupid*," the girls hissed before she was dragged away. She sat inside the room with the hot wet smell of sex and pain and fear and she knew they were right. Maybe she'd just thrown everything away, maybe she'd thrown away her chance to be free.

The Kahn Warrior let in the first creature and Mae scrambled to her feet and backed across the room. No one answered her screams. No one came when she clawed at the bed and kicked and the creature slammed her head into the wall until she let go, swam loose inside herself but not far enough inside to get away from the pain.

The second creature only wanted her to scream. He traced her muscles, her nerves, he touched her the way the very first creature she'd been given to had, setting her very blood alight.

She knew she was going to die in that room that night.

She longed for the simple grace of execution.

The third creature had a spot of color taking up one-quarter of his eye. He caught her when she fell away from the wall and eased her onto the bed. He covered her and stroked her hair and sent her visions and let her cry. He took the privilege of the room for the rest of the night and woke her before the soldiers came to take her back. Just before the door swung open he forced out, "Promise me. You'll run."

"What did they do to you?" Oona covered for her in the kitchen that day. She kept Mae out of sight and mashed up what food she could find into a disgusting mix that yet was warm and thick and comforting.

Mae's throat hurt, though she couldn't remember anyone hitting her there. Her head ached and her ribs made her gasp for air. Past that were the bruises. The new girls gave her wide berth, as if she might be contagious, which angered Oona who had watched Mae feed them when they were hurt, and amused Mae, who thought she might have done the same thing in their places. She was long-term now, one of the longest lasting girls, and she didn't have much longer. If one of them didn't kill her, then all of them would tire of her. It was time to go.

She didn't know how.

The Kahn Warrior who dragged her to the Silent Barracks the night before dragged her to line up late that afternoon. Oona hissed in fury and Mae closed her eyes at her, the closest she could come to saying *it's all right, don't get hurt over it*. She moved wherever they pushed or pulled her, keeping her right side turned away, the pocket of her shift sagging under the weight of a paring knife stolen from the kitchens. No one ever thought to keep knives from the girls. No one thought much about the girls at all. Who thinks about the enemy after it is conquered?

The soldier who chose her was a new captain, glorying in his rank, brutal as any creature had ever dreamed of being.

"What's your name?"

*What would you like it to be?* That would be safest. Followed by a simple answer. "Mae."

"That's not a name. It's a month." He waited to see if she'd take offense. How much sport would she be?

Mae didn't care if he made fun of her name. The ones who talked, nicely or not, were a nuisance. *Get it over with.* "What's your name?" As if she cared.

"What's it to you, bitch?"

*That's a stupid name*, she could have said in retaliation for his comment. She didn't answer. She stood still in the middle of the room because he hadn't told her to do anything else yet. His parka had a name tag that read Captain James Crawford.

"You can call me Capt. Crawford," he said suddenly, sounding very damn proud of that captain thing. He was, she realized, very drunk, more drunk than most of the men got on Altarus. Drunk too often translated into dead drunk – literally, because men would pass out and freeze to death.

But Captain James Crawford had been celebrating. Currently he was trying to remove his standard issue military boots without untying them, pulling harder on the bottom of the boot until Mae expected his foot to come off along with the boot and the captain slowly and ignonimously rolled backward like a child's toy.

She schooled her face to impersonal concern but only took one step in his direction before he stopped her. "Never mind, I'm all right, take off that stupid dress."

She went still and cold. *Last time*, she told herself. Whatever happened, this was the last time. If she made it out alive. Or if she didn't. The paring knife made the dress sag on one side. What of it? The men weren't here to study women's war time prison fashions.

She slid the dress over her head, instantly chilled in a lower rank room. Before the shift could slither down to the floor she caught it and eased it down, the knife still inside the pocket. If only he would hurry and undress. She didn't want to have to do it herself. She didn't want bloody clothes, either, and she eyed his jacket again, a shirt-waist but that was all right, it would be longer on her and it was waterproof and fur-lined with a fur-lined hood. She could almost feel it on her now. "Let me help you."

Amazement showed on his face. Comfort women might have the fight beaten out of them but they did not offer to help their attackers undress.

"Anxious, are you?" He attempted something of a leer. His shirt came off finally, a thermal that reeked of a dislike for the laundering practices on Altarus. Mae wrinkled her nose at it, then tugged at the cuffs of his pants. "Just hold on, would you?"

*You're going to blow it.*

She couldn't stop. Slim, lithe, beautiful, 19. Angry, trapped, beaten, her creamy skin a rainbow of new and used bruises. She turned his cuffs loose and bent and picked up the discarded shirt. It was still warm. Sliding it over her head was like climbing into the pelt recently stripped from the animal who had previously owned it. "How do I look?"

"Like a dumb bitch who's about to get her ass kicked." Mae's touching his stuff had made him seriously angry. She'd be in trouble if only he could stand up. She bent down and grabbed his cuffs again. This time she pulled hard, yanking the pants over his hips and down his legs and off his body in three hard pulls.

The young captain was slim and strong. Mae was curvy and young. The jeans fit tight across her hips, didn't touch her waist.

They'd do. She took his socks. She took his too-big boots. She took his anorak with the badge that proclaimed she was now Captain James Crawford.

He got to his feet then, and started making threatening sounds. The knife slipped between his ribs easier than she could ever have expected. So this was what it was like to cause the hurt.

She took his life. She took his keys. She took his sidearm. She used the keys and opened the cell door and walked out into the cold, bleak afternoon.

They'd been in one of the rooms closest to the outside. It made some kind of sense to have the hood up before she got out of the building.

Nobody looked twice at her.

The cold was still like a blow, but better in Captain James' fur-lined jacket. She cursed because he hadn't any gloves in the pockets and what idiot went around on Altarus without gloves if he had them?  Curse turned to giggle.  For maybe the first time since they brought her to Altarus, Mae laughed.  He'd stored rations in his pockets.  Raisins.  A hard roll.  Packets of peanuts.  A candy bar.

She didn't have time for this and she didn't care.  For five minute Mae crouched in the shadows, hid and feasted.

The sunlight stretched long across the frozen outpost.  She didn't expect guards.  There was nowhere to go on Altarus.  No one was stupid enough to run.

For an instant she hesitated.  Perched at the edge of a series of steel transport containers.  Pain drummed through her ribs and stomach.  Cold ate at her hands inside the jacket sleeves.  Brittle ice lay over everything, dazzling, throwing back prisms of light, refracting off individual crystals.  The trees lay ahead of her, and within them, one of the gaps where the trees had been hacked aside to create paths.

Maybe no one really did run.  Maybe the doctor had lied to her, set her up for sport.  Maybe the cock-sure young Captain James was a plant, a troublemaker the others were willing to sacrifice.  But she remembered the doctor's eyes.  The way she'd glanced over her shoulder and then held her voice steady, talking low but refusing to whisper.

There was no other choice.  The captain would be missed.  His rank was low – he couldn't have rated more than a couple hours with a comfort woman.

The sun slid another notch in the alien sky and the path in front of her lit, clear as a map.  Not the path she'd been staring at, but off to the side, heading southwest, exactly as the doctor had said, a thinning of some trees.  Nothing that would be seen if someone didn't know to look.

If she got lost, if she got it wrong, if the doctor had lied, she'd die out here.

But she'd die without someone hitting her. She'd die with the captain's rations in her stomach. She'd die on her own terms. She was very much against it, but going back meant torture, execution, death. The doctor had told her there was a place. Cold, harsh, hard, but full of women and they would welcome her. She just had to reach out for cold comfort.

*The working title for Sound of Wind in Wires was, simply, Clinic. At the time I wrote the story I'd been doing some freelance work for a community foundation that was engaged in doing a lot of good in Reno. Many of their ideas and ideals embraced positive change and philanthropic concepts. But for my tastes, they went a step too far. Which got me thinking about what happens when those who can help choose to "help" those who don't want – or need – help. It's about fixing problems where problems don't exist.*

# The Sound of Wind in Wires

Clinic, day 56. Felt like way more than almost two months. Damn long days on this planet. Ever since he arrived summer's been deepening, longer and longer days and all Jax wants to do is kick back and drink beer and do nothing. Or maybe it's the camping out effect of being somewhere so recently colonized. If you want to call Rigel colonized. It's just the oil company roughnecks, the service providers, the hookers and the clinic making up the human population on the planet. Earth class planet with Earth class fossil fuels and nobody but the archeological/anthropological faction cares what the fuel is fossilized *from*, but these people care a lot and show up every time Univers-Oil tries to drill somewhere new. Them and the tree huggers and the Indigenous Peoples Rights Groups, so it's not just one happy little family any more. Jump technology's made it easy to travel, so everybody does.

Clinic, day 56, and he's been waiting almost two months

for one of them to come in. Waiting without realizing he was. Ever since the lunatic flyboy crash landed the scooter at the transfer point and Daniel picked him up for the ride into town he's been waiting.

Town. Or something. Indigenous peoples don't really to go in for towns. They've got settlements but nothing humans recognize as towns. It might be backwards, it might not be PC, it might be just plain damn wrong, but Jax doesn't consider it a town if he can't get beer and pizza.

He doesn't know why he ever let Mare convince him to come here. All that talk about his talent working in clinics and programs at home. It went to his head. For a while he tried arguing with her. There are people on Earth in need of clinics and programs, that's why those things exist and he was trained to work in them. But Mare needed to get away, out of Philly and off past the moon, out of the galaxy and into the big, bright beyond that waited full of adventure and it would be even better between them then and c'mon, Jax, let's *go*. What was he going to say to a six foot statuesque blonde other than Yes?

Goodbye. It was likely he'd say goodbye. Less than two months on Rigel and Mare had already admitted she hated it and she'd made a mistake and all she wanted to do was go home where she could take her shoes off outside without fear of running into burrowing nettles that spread infection through the entire body and where, for that matter, they had shoe shops that sold shoes, pretty shoes, not boots, places like Sak's and somehow or another that entire argument ended up being about shoes and Sak's and Jax was able to convince himself it would be just as good if she went home, or at least he told himself he was convinced.

The door to the clinic hissed open and it entered. It. PC was to call them TG. TransGendered. Jax didn't know anybody who called them that when Admin wasn't looking, except maybe Admin himself, tight ass little creep of the dot every I in triplicate variety. Everyone else called them Its. Only right now the super smooth white brow over startling red-brown eyes led to a feminine face and a very definite female body. She'd bred, and the breeding produced pregnancy and for now, she was a female.

Jax realized he hadn't said anything yet, was just standing and staring and he shut his mouth with a snap. Third sex. Third gender. Neuters. Daniel had pointed them out on the way to the clinic, pointed out as well some of the places in the settlement they frequented. Third sex until mating, then the results of the mating determined their sex; male, and they went out and performed again; female only because they were pregnant.

He managed to drag his gaze off her stomach and meet her eyes. She looked faintly amused. "My pairbond sent me here," she said without waiting for him to ask if he could help her. The IP had learned Earth tongues within days. Humans hadn't returned the favor by learning the guttural, clicking language of the IP. The green activists and sociologists were trying. The Clinic workers fumbled with badly assembled dictionaries. The oil company roughnecks simply shot at them if they came too close.

"What can I help you with?" Jax finally managed and his voice came out high, squeaky and jumpy, not at all the way he wanted it to sound.

It– she– frowned. "Not me. My pairbond. They're the ones who wanted me to come."

It was never good when they were still in denial about the problem; it made it so much harder to treat.

"They gave me this," she said and held out the laminated plastic card she'd been toying with. The IP didn't go in for pockets, purses or backpacks. The card was warm from her hands. Jax would code it for her, no way to fake the code, and whoever had sent her would know she'd been there. He felt on firmer ground now. Less than two months but he'd seen enough cases this was becoming routine.

"Come in, sit." He motioned at the plastic chairs, bright orange, same things they'd have on Earth, always canted the person seated in them into an anxious position as if they might bolt at any minute.

She looked like she might.

"Can I get you some coffee?" he asked and then winced. Habit. Cure one addiction with another. They'd been asked not to introduce the IP to Earth addictions. Caffeine. Nicotine. Sugar. She shook her head anyway. "I'm Jax," he told her and poured a plastic tumbler of Rigel's water, so full of minerals you could stand a toothbrush upright in the stuff. Handed her the glass and sat down behind the desk across from her. She stared at the glass as if she couldn't decide what to do with it and settled for placing it on the edge of his desk.

"_____," she said, a series of sounds he could never reproduce, something like a cat purring and something like nature in overload or transports downshifting on the freeways back home. She smiled briefly then and said, "Call me Ty."

"Ty," Jax repeated. "What brings you to the clinic, Ty?" he asked and waited for her to tell him again her pairbond had sent her. The other two IP she had mated with, formed a family that would stay together until the child was born. Sexed, and it would stay with the couple. Neuter, and it would go with Ty.

Instead of repeating herself she leaned back in the hard plastic chair, her feet splayed out in front of her and put her hands on her stomach. "They've been saying that 'catl isn't healthy for offspring, even before they're born." She used the IP term for achtonacatl, something Jax had figured out after only a few minutes at the clinic. Use was widespread– planet wide. And Earth thought it had problems with crystal meth. He watched her, waiting for her to go on. Sooner or later she'd make a statement someone else hadn't said to her; something he could work with. "They say it stimulates the nervous systems and causes us to live too fast."

It was a rough translation, and good enough. Jax nodded. Around him the clinic was silent. Midday, usually empty, the other social workers had headed out for food, sometimes a good search because not all of the so-called human restaurants were really restaurants and not all of them really served human food and not all of them were open when they said they were. Inside the clinic was sterile white, too much empty space between cubicles that were stupidly arranged so counselors had to stand to see the door. Sterile white, nothing like the IP's habitats. Outside the sunlight stretched long and hot. If he closed his eyes he could be back on Earth listening to any of a thousand expectant mothers– it's only marijuana, cocaine, herbal supplements, caffeine, alcohol, one drink, two, it's not a big deal, not in my case– but when he opened them again the expectant mother would have a light pattern of scales across her cheeks and hands, pale skin despite the summer sun and a fall of white hair that traveled down below her waist, twining with darker hair from her vertebrae.

Jax realized she'd stopped talking and tried to backtrack. Shameful to be caught not listening. He could only go far enough back to realize her last words had ended on an upbeat– a question.

"I'm sorry, I–"

"You weren't listening." She pressed her lips together tightly, the way the IP smiled. "You hear this all day."

Actually, it had been a quiet week, quiet days that balanced out the increasingly loud and angry nights with Mare.

"What I said was, I don't understand <u>when</u> 'catl became dangerous." She folded her hands over her rounded stomach like any other pregnant woman in the Universe and Jax opened and closed his mouth several times, at a loss for words.

But this is what he had trained for. He was a counselor, a professional. This was what he did. Abruptly he was back again and he stood, pacing, the same way he'd lecture a DUI class on Earth, or a smoke stoppers session for expectant parents, or a methadone group. "Achtonacatl effects the central nervous systems," he said, enumerating on his fingers and remembering to plural system. The IP operated with a bilateral CNS. 'Catl grabbed both of them in a headlock and wrestled sense from them. Brain sent out messages through the spinal column and out through the rest of the body and from there the drug seemed to vanish- no one could find it in the body any more, just the effects: some nausea, dilated pupils, increase in pulse, blood pressure and temperature, rapid speech and thought. There was a sense of peace as well as a sense of excitement, as if everything that was happening was good and positive and wonderful. Like the manic half of bipolar disorder, 'catl users talked fast and moved faster. They made decisions quickly, ate quickly, talked quickly and laughed at everything. At higher doses they hallucinated, believing they transcended. Time and space suspended and the IP joined in their planet's spiral orbital dance, becoming a part of the everything around them, a part of Rigel, their sentient world.

The IP loved Rigel, their families and their Ancestors. They were intelligent, non-materialistic and peaceful, and their too-peaceful resistance to the oil companies and the drilling led to the oil companies simply walking over them in the time honored tradition of Conquest. Which led to the tangles of Indigenous Peoples and roughnecks– achtonacatl seemed most plentiful at drill sites. Use of the drug was so widespread it was assumed by survey teams to involve fully 95 percent of the IP without regard for age, gender, responsibility within the community– or pregnancy.

When Earth teams started traveling to Rigel they were preceded by teams of world government analysts and sociologists who determined contact with the IP was unavoidable. They were smart, sentient and everywhere. It was determined that first contact with humans wouldn't prove harmful to the IP and might even be beneficial. And thus the drilling started and the service providers followed and once the widespread problem of addiction was determined, the clinics began spreading as well.

Jax fumbled and caught himself. "Achtonacatl is a drug," he said. He could have named any one of a hundred substances; here it was 'catl. "It changes both physical and mental conditions and responses." She was watching him but he couldn't tell what she was thinking. Abruptly he felt foolish, pacing and lecturing to his audience of one. He spun the chair around and dropped down onto it, straddling it, forearms resting along the top. "Achtonacatl is a central nervous system stimulant. Once in the system it begins making a variety of changes to the user."

Ty nodded. "Rapid heartbeat. Rapid speech. Big eyes."

Jax held his hands out, encouraging, and Ty obligingly continued. In another direction. "It also brings us closer to what your people know as the godhead. As religion? The soul. Under to everything changes. The–" she mimed with her hands, outlining along the sides of her face as if she were wearing blinders– "The separation changes," she substituted.

"It causes hallucinations," Jax said firmly. "In high enough doses it causes the chemicals in the brain to misfire. Neurotransmitters overload and the user hallucinates." Studies had been done on human subjects– only a few, and heavily regulated– and on the limited number of IP who were willing to come forward. "The user believes–"

She leaned forward and placed one hand on his forearm. Jax was always surprised at how cool the skin of the IP was but Ty's hand was burning. "No," she said. She looked into his eyes as if searching for something she could work with to convince him. As if Jax were being counseled, tables suddenly turned. "Have you ever had a moment when everything was right?" she asked at last. "Where you could close your eyes and feel the light from the star across your shoulders and know that everything was going the way it should, that your life was unfolding gradually and sweetly and that there was no fear and no pain, just a rightness? A moment when you knew everything was just as it should be?"

Hallucination. Vision. Pleasant enough but brought about by the screw up of brain chemicals, and he opened his mouth to say so but Ty spoke first.

"Have you ever felt fully loved? Loved and that you belonged, a part of everything, without having to do a single other thing than just be?"

Jax stared at her, mouth open, brain empty, trying to process a rush of emotions that made him feel weak. "It's not–" he started and was saved from having to figure out what he meant to say when the door to the clinic flew open. Daniel came through, moving fast, eyes wide and hands still out in front of him as if to push through more doors. Darlene was right behind him, and Charlynn. Counselors running and Jax started up out of his chair. Ty flinched away from him and turned to look at the others.

"C'mon," Daniel said. He was already across the room and fumbling at the locked cabinets, he could never remember the combination, not even when he wasn't panicked and Jax said "39, 15, 6" without thinking. Darlene stiffened but moved past him to another cabinet. They'd have to change the codes now. The IP weren't allowed access to human weapons.

"Catch," Daniel said. The taser flipped end over end and Jax caught it almost by mistake.

"What the hell are you doing?"

"There's an incident," Darlene said. She was halfway to the door. "Cross town. We are *not* having another repeat of Mile High."

Jax started for the door before he remembered Ty. He still needed to do her intake, get her assigned to a group, get himself set up as her counselor. What had he <u>been</u> doing? "I need you to stay–"

She was right behind him; he was almost yelling into her face. Jax put both hands on her shoulders, right hand awkwardly holding the taser away from her. "You need to stay here."

Ty opened her mouth wide, IP version of a scream. "It's <u>my</u> home," she said simply and moved more fluidly than any pregnant woman on any planet should have been able to, slipped around him and headed for the door. Jax stood still, just long enough to decide whether to curse or sigh or smile. When he hit the door he was running. He passed Ty and joined the counselors, threw himself into the last spot in the back of the transport just before the pseudo truck lurched into life, ploughing through heat and dust toward Drill Site 327, Mesa Verde.

Just before she was out of site Jax saw Ty looking after them and saw the shutters come down over her face.

Drill site 327 was situated in a beautiful valley 15 kilometers or so from the clinic. One of the biggest producers so far, Univers-Oil was pulling mega amounts of fuel out of the ground. The site was promising enough for the town to start forming. It was one of the reasons the clinic had set up here, one of the reasons Jax had come, he and Mare both, Mare doing double duty or maybe triple, serving as Univers-Oil's accountant at this site of the planet, keeping their software up and running and tracking everything that came in and went out. She'd be here, simple blue suit in among the orange coveralls, yelling as loudly as the roughnecks. Jax started looking for her the minute the transport came over the hill and began dropping into the valley. Blue green grass under the tires, and they drove between leafy stick-trunked trees that grew high and thin with leaves reaching for the fat, endless sky overhead. Hills rolled smoothly down into the valley and some distance away started up again, leading to distant mountains. It was a valley meant for anything but the grasshopper-looking cranes that dug into the ground at neatly spaced intervals. Heavy equipment, dark metal and burnt orange coveralls. The valley belonged to Univers-Oil, they'd bought it, land claim, advertised and got no responses or objections. Never mind the IP didn't read much Earth English or that there was no one to buy it from because no one on Rigel understood the concept of owning pieces of the planet– Univers-Oil understood it, Univers-Oil owned it and the IP standing there today were standing there illegally on Univers-Oil's soil. Arrayed against them stood the activists and next to them the anthropologists and archeologists, everyone wearing the same expressions of distrust, dislike, betrayal and helpless fury.

The transport lumbered to a stop at the summit of the hill. Jax jumped down onto the grass.

He let out a sigh when he saw Mare wasn't among them, caught his breath again when he took in the situation. A crew of roughnecks, some 15 or more men– sunburnt, oilburnt, scruffy and rough– and all of them armed. They carried rifles and handguns to a man and they'd backed the IP up against a stand of thick low trees, ringed them until retreat was impossible, then ordered them off Univers-Oil's land.

The yelling had started a while ago from the look of it. Even the IP were yelling, mouths open and teeth bared, long-fingered hands waving. The roughnecks waved their guns in response. Jax rubbed one hand over his face and when he looked up again he saw Mare across the site. She stood in the mix of roughnecks and suits, her face tight and angry. She hadn't seen him yet.

"Damn it," Jax said but before he could move Darlene brushed past him.

"This doesn't have to be a problem here," she said, her hands held out soothingly, her voice perfectly audible but forcibly calm. "If we all work together—"

Jax saw Daniel cringe at clinic-speak before the crew chief glanced once at Darlene, braced the rifle against his hip and fired a warning shot into the air. Barely into the air. Jax thought it had come closer than anyone had expected. Darlene didn't have enough sense to stop until the guy pointed the weapon directly at her.

"Lady, this is none of your business. Why don't you and your little friends go back to whatever elevated consciousness you crawled out of and let us handle our own business?"

"Your business doesn't include harassing the IP," Darlene said, and her voice rose a notch. "There is no reason—"

"Lady, they're on our land in front of our site," the chief said and the nearest and tallest of the IP stepped forward and said, "It's our site. This is a sacred—"

The butt of the rifle crushed his cheekbone. From across the field Jax could hear the bone splinter. He was in motion before he thought about it. So was everyone else.

Darlene went down first. Her taser flew out of her hand and she doubled and dropped when one of the crew slammed his rifle into her stomach. Jax took a step to the side, confused— there were too many people around and he half wanted to go to Mare or Darlene and half wanted to back off and some other very logical part of his brain was sending messages like "There's no way out of this" and "Get your hands up" which he did, in time to deflect a blow aimed at his head but not a second fist that came out of nowhere and connected soundly with his cheekbone just below his left eye. Jax shouted, surprise and fury at once. Somewhere nearby he heard Daniel yell. The IP were moving too, everything starting to blur and he wasted precious seconds wondering wasn't he supposed to speed up or time slow down or something when someone sucker punched him in the kidneys and Rigel went red. He'd never had any formal training, it just seemed to come as naturally as the need to help did. Skinned his knuckles on one man's jaw, felt bearded stubble and flesh and the guy kept going. Jax grabbed him again, knee to abdomen and when the man swung at him, knee to groin and he spun looking: Who's next? Darlene's taser lay on the ground a few feet away. He lunged at it but someone kicked it out of his hand, Jax pulled back, hot fire ache in his fingers, hand, wrist, forearm, it *cannot* be broken and someone spun him, Jax's hands going up, Daniel let go and they stood together for an instant as roughnecks and IP grappled; the IP would grab and cling and pull their opponents down except then another Univers-Oil roughneck would pummel them from behind.

Back on his feet, moving toward two roughnecks battering a female IP, Jax saw Mare across from him. She had her datacom out, was yelling into the thing and scrawling the stylus across the screen and even now Jax could hear the low whup whup of choppers. Turned. Someone kicked Darlene. He saw Daniel grab the guy and the man elbowed Daniel in the face. The clinic worker down in a spray of blood, roughneck bending over him, followed him down with fist cocked, Daniel thin and bearded and *down*, damn it, no longer a threat. Jax got within arm's length of the guy, *take a swing, bring him down* but the world lit up, every fiber of his being, every nerve, every muscle awake and screaming in pain and he shuddered, jolted, saw Mare standing across from him holding a weapon drawn on two IP, she didn't even look at him and he was out.


"We do *not* engage. This is *not* why we're here. You people have violated so many regulations I could have you sent back to Earth, stripped of your licenses, locked up and the keys thrown away and I still wouldn't even have <u>started</u>."

Admin paced, forward and back, too fast like a caged cat and late day sun splintered as he moved. *Frizzy. Fuzzy. Fussy. Frilly.* Jax had gotten to the F's, Adjectives for Admin. Anything to stop the nausea, to distract him from the afternoon and the lingering effects of the taser. And from the thought of going home, for that matter.

Jax ached. Every bone, every muscle. A couple of teeth felt loose. After the roughneck had broken the IP's face events had fast forwarded. Darlene walked into the gun and the chief fired close enough to move her hair, right before she tasered him and kept the trigger depressed until another 'neck clubbed her with a handgun and one of the IP stepped forward and then everyone stepped up until it was a blur, IP and humans, roughnecks and clinic workers and the sounds of breaking bones and human rage and it wasn't until the police arrived– and then a little while past– that it all stopped.

When Jax surfaced from his thoughts the Admin was still pacing and still spewing. He looked around the empty sterile clinic and saw Mare just beyond the door.

Jax groaned. She was waiting. She would continue to

wait. She'd accompany him home, back to their lodgings whether he liked it or not. For all he knew he could be in her custody now. Certainly Mare would see it that way.

He closed his eyes and leaned back in the chair and hoped Admin had more to say. Much more.

"How could you do that? What were you thinking? You put my *job* at risk." Mare paced their tiny living room, six steps and double back. His day for listening to people rant and watching them pace. Jax put both hands on his head, palms pressing against his temples, and wondered if he could stop it from detonating. The way it hurt he assumed not.

"Jax. Are you listening to me? This is my *job* we're talking about." She stopped pacing and stood over him. Making sure he was listening. Or properly repentant.

"Your job." He could feel heat crawl across the back of his shoulders. "*Your. Job.*" He stood, suddenly enough Mare backed off two steps. "Your. Job." He moved past her and stood at the window. There was nothing to see outside. There never was. This was a quiet planet. Or it had been. There were trees and birds and the night sky with its confusing un-Earth stars. For just a second Jax wanted desperately to see a dipper, big or small, he could never tell them apart anyway or remember which he was looking at. "Mare. Your job. What about mine? My career? What about what I came here to do?" When he looked up at her, she was staring.

"Your car-eeer. Oh. Yes. Of course. I forgot about that. You came here—"

"I came here to help," Jax said. He wanted to make her stop talking so he wouldn't have to hear the sneer in her voice.

"You came here because of <u>me</u>," Mare said and now she sounded ragged and close to tears. Jax turned and looked at her. Mare cried when she was cornered, but she wasn't so much cornered here as lost. Mare wasn't about exploration or new worlds. Mare was corporate. Mare was Sak's. Mare was a halfway expensive bottle of wine at a good restaurant after a play.

"Mare, I'm sorry. What happened today–" He reached for her and she jerked back like he meant to hit her.

"They were *there*, Jax," she shouted. Her fists balled at her sides. Before he could ask she said, "Top executives. CEO's. CFO's. CTO's. They were *there*. We came here for *my* career, we came here so <u>I</u> could advance. And *they* come and *they* see *you*. See you siding with *them*."

He didn't ask what she meant. She trembled. He doubted she could see him. Mare was a supernova in process, everything turned inward.

"What happened today was wrong," he said gently. Let her take it any way she chose. "What happened today–"

"Was *your* fault." She spun on him. "Them. The precious *indigenous peoples*. Them and their filthy, filthy drugs!"

Sometime just before the planet's long dawn she came and sat on the arm of his chair. Jax had spent the night there, scrolling through movie titles on the monitor. He thought there might be a couple million movies listed and still there wasn't anything he wanted to watch. She put her hand on his arm as if she were afraid he wouldn't acknowledge she was there. When he met her eyes she moved her hand to the side of his face, so light a touch she didn't even hurt the bruises there.

"I'm sorry. Jax. I am. I don't think you wanted to come

here." She shook her head when he tried to interrupt. "I don't think you're responsible for Them." She took a deep breath and he heard the shake in it. "I just hate it here and when they do that." She stopped. Breathe, breathe, breathe, like a mantra. He could imagine her saying it. "It's not like we want the whole planet." She wasn't looking at his face anymore; she looked at a neutral spot somewhere past his right ear.

"It's not like they owe us *any* part of the planet," he said. Everything hurt. He felt like he was still being tasered. He missed the look in her eyes but he heard it in her voice.

"It's *Univers-Oil's* land."

"Oh, come on, Mare, how can it be? The IP don't even believe in owning land. So how could they sell it? How could Univers-Oil own it? How could the IP even understand Univers-Oil thinks the land is theirs? The concept doesn't even make sense to them!"

"Does it have to make sense? Do they have to understand? Can't they just– go?"

"Go where?" He pushed past her, leveraged himself out of the chair. "And it wasn't just any site. There are drill sites the IP never go near. This was a sacred site. It's sacred to them, Mare, don't you get it?"

She turned back to him and said hard and fast, "It's sacred to them because of their damn drugs." Paused for no more than a heartbeat but he already thought he knew what she was going to say. "Aren't you supposed to take care of that?"

The clinic opened the next day at seven a.m., same as always.

A handful of IP came in for group, led by Daniel and

Charlynn. One of the more voluntary groups, where members had Embraced their Need to Change and come forward on their own. Admitting there is a problem is the first step and all that. He resented that Charlynn had drawn that group. She was a large frazzled woman with weapons-grade fingernails who seemed to sullenly dislike anyone with a substance abuse problem. Jax thought it would be fair to stick Charlynn with the groups of involuntary IP, the ones whose family units had sent them. Groups of sullen, unresponsive aliens who seemed to dislike anyone who tried to help them with their problem.

Jax spent the morning doing paperwork, putting together names for new groups and working a little on the clinic schedule. Helping Admin with that chore meant not only brownie points but a much more reasonable schedule for everyone involved. By lunch the clinic had been empty a couple hours— voluntary IP came and went early, back to their days after the interruption. The involuntary IP weren't coming today. Not after the incident at Mesa Verde. The counselors went to lunch together. Daniel lingered at the door. "You coming?"

Jax looked up from his monitor. "I'll stay. Someone might come."

Daniel shook his head. "Not today. We could probably close if it wasn't for." He shrugged and nodded at Admin's empty office. Jax ran through potential excuses— just in case, paperwork, getting caught up— and said, "I'm just not feeling sociable today."

Daniel wasn't phased. His face as black and blue above his brown beard and one shoulder hunched higher than the other as if something hurt enough to require holding it rigid. "Bring you back a sandwich."

"Great."

After Daniel went the clinic was almost silent. Inside and outside matched– white hot. The sterile white clinic, the empty white-hot streets. Jax logged onto the network and started scrolling for news flashes. More reports from anthropologists, speculating on a mass extinction in rather recent Rigel history. Like Earth, there had been dinosaurs; those were the fossils the scientists hunted. And like Earth, there had been meteors. Unlike Earth, however, it was speculated the dinosaurs were intelligent, capable of forming a society, and most of them very likely had scaled flesh.

Jax stopped reading and scrolled again. Not what he was looking for. He was looking for creatures who were not at rest and there they were, reports of several incidents the previous day across the planet, all at drill sites.

Jax looked at the reports, each with a paragraph lead description after and frowned. He tapped the monitor, rearranged the display so only the headlines remained. Five reported incidents with indigenous peoples the day before. He narrowed it again. Four were at drill sites; the fifth was in a tiny, three-bar town, IP and roughnecks. He rearranged the order again, searched by keyword. Find "Sacred." It came up in all five reports. Four incidents, including the one at Drill Site 327, Mesa Verde, that involved drill sites sacred to the IP, the incident between IP and roughnecks, was over a site being drilled, it simply took place somewhere else.

"They consider the whole damn planet sacred," one Univers-Oil employee who asked to remain nameless was quoted as saying. "It's like the Native Americans on Earth– any time anyone wants to do anything anywhere there they are, saying it's a sacred big juju place."

Jax figured right after he stopped talking the man spit

into the dirt and shouldered some kind of weapon-like machinery before turning and walking back to his buddies. He could be right– maybe they were just throwing up sacred spaces in the face of Univers-Oil in the hopes of making drilling impossible. If so, Jax couldn't say he blamed them. On the other hand, no government or administrative body had seen fit to honor any sacred sites. The creed seemed to be we don't want the whole planet so stop being selfish and go pursue your religion somewhere else.

The crossover of sites just seemed– significant.

The clinic doors opened and let in a blast of heat. Too soon for Daniel and the others to be back and Jax hoped unfaithfully it wasn't Mare.

The IP stood framed against the white light and then the door closed behind her and Jax blinked, eyes dazzled. "Ty?"

"Did they all run away and leave you?" She slid into a chair across the desk from him and perched uncomfortably, as dictated by the chair. Jax got up and rolled over Daniel's desk chair, indicated she should take it.

"Looks like they did." He wasn't sure what to say to her. He'd seen her at the site. She'd arrived late with a group of IP. Today she was untouched and Jax looked like a Jack-o-lantern come to rest on All Saint's Day after having been kicked down the road a piece by local goblins.

"Who hit you?" She leaned forward like she might touch him and Jax found himself leaning toward her rather than away, but Ty just looked.

"Who didn't?" It came out meaner than he meant it to.

"The Saith," Ty said at once, using the IP's own form of address. "Not one of them."

She let it sink in for a minute and Jax finally nodded. His damage was all manmade. He didn't say anything though and after a moment Ty leaned back, then stood and moved away from him, across the completely empty clinic and to the door. He thought she might leave altogether .

"We don't hit. Usually. We know. You're only trying to help." She faced him then and added, "You're wrong, but you're trying to help."

He signed her up then, for two group sessions every week, one on understanding and one on breaking addiction. With the pregnancy and the fact that they didn't understand IP physiology very well yet he couldn't sign her up for yoga or any other exercise class, but he could and did put himself in place as her counselor, then walked her over to the other side of the building for bloodwork, which freaked all IP, and back again.

"I didn't expect you to come back," he said as he offered her a reminder card with times and dates. Ty declined. She had nowhere to carry it. She'd remember. She was already carrying around the plastic laminate clinic card. Jax waited now for her to mention her pairbond, or pick up and leave, or tell him it was some arrangement reached with planetary security after the Mesa Verde incident.

Ty put her hands over her stomach, explaining rather than protecting. "I've never done this before. I don't know what to expect. The Saith have been on Rigel forever. It's our homeworld. But we have only been intwined with achtonacatl for our ancestors' ancestors' ancestors' time." She stopped briefly and just looked at him and Jax knew the thrill of success he'd feel on Earth when a first time mother put her addiction aside for her child's sake.

That rush of feeling didn't come.

When Jax said nothing, Ty continued. "Only in the last few years have we seen an increase in wounded births. But why take the chance? When my child is born I can always return to achtonacatl. If I choose. I will miss it, I know that."

He wanted to ask her then how she knew it was her child she carried– perhaps as a neuter she'd give birth to a sexed child that would stay with the pairbond. He wanted to ask her what the experience was like, what changes the drug unleashed, why the IP chose to believe they walked with their ancestors when using, what the tie in between the sacred sites and Univers-Oil's drill sites was. He thought he might already know.

"Ty–"

The clinic door opened; all at once heat and light and parts of a couple conversations flowed in, Daniel arguing with Charlynn about something, *Here's your sandwich, old man, and believe it or not found you a Coke, if you don't want it I'll– oh, sorry, sorry, didn't know, excuse me–* and he was out again and around them the other conversations continued, louder now as counselors made their way to individual desks. Ty just watched him, and then she watched his coke. Jax didn't ask, just opened the can and handed it to her and the hell with the idea they were going to somehow mess up the IP with caffeine or sugar.

"Next day," Ty said and she was gone.

He logged onto the network and went looking for sites where the anthropologists were working. There were a couple dozen active sites logged, most of them corresponding to– or even holding up– Univers-Oil drill sites. Had always made sense, before– drill sites were limited time access. Move fast or they'd fall prey to progress. He'd never questioned it. Jax thought about overlaying the map of sacred sites, decided not to waste the time. He canceled his afternoon group (in light of the previous day, Admin was apocalyptic.) He was out the door and on his way.

The site was quiet today. Just grass, trees, sand and anthropologists. Nothing like Mesa Verde had been the day before. He'd come to the closest site he could find. Now he was here he wasn't sure what to do next. It already looked like a drill site: big hole in the ground, guys in hard hats poking around in it. But there were more women here doing the same things as the men and instead of heavy machinery people were using hand shovels and whisk brooms.

Jax hung back. Around him the afternoon simmered. Nothing moved in the trees– no wind, no birds stupid enough to waste energy on a day this hot. Humans, though. Humans were willing, hydrating every few seconds, breathing in dust and who knew what microbes or bacteria– they didn't know enough about the planet to be working unprotected but it was too hot for masks. Still they moved at a good pace, quick as they could without risking samples. Finds were labeled, documented, and moved. There was never any way of knowing just when UO would move in to *their* new site or who the whimsical circuit court would side with this time.

Past the hole in the ground everything was beautiful. Barren and still. This part of the planet sported long vistas of waving grasses, chest high in some places and, he'd heard, at some times of year it was full of tiny biting insects. Deep summer it was home to somnolent mammals and a few non-lethal snakes. When the wind blew most of the time it was silent but occasionally it made a high pitched whine, the way wind on Earth sounded through the high wires. Jax remembered the first time he'd jolted aware, realizing he'd accepted the sound was wind in wires and coming to because there were no wires here. Popular theory held the sound was wind through conical leaves which made the sound of a certain bird, attracting the bird's hopeful suitors who, disappointed, would stay and eat the tree fruit and do the tree's replanting.

There was so much here. So much past—

"Can I help you?"

Jax jolted and caught himself. The voice came from somewhere near his knees. When he looked, the woman's head and shoulders were above the rim of the pit.

"I said, can I help you?" She sounded irritated.

"I heard you," Jax said. "You startled me."

The woman rolled her eyes and heaved herself out of the pit in one fluid motion. She straightened, dusted and inspected Jax critically. "You don't *look* like a wildcatter," she said.

Jax, nonplused, said, "Should I?"

Instead of answering directly the woman snapped her fingers and said, "Clinic boy. I smoke pot and drink beer at night after a long day out here. You want to fix <u>me</u>?"

"What? No." There were standard responses for this sort of thing— whether it came from other humans or from IP thinking a double standard existed or whatever the source— but confusion drummed it out of Jax's brain. He'd intended to watch, wait, find a chance to slip down and recover a bit of fossil. It had all seemed to make some kind of sense back when he left the clinic.

She was still watching him as if she suspected him of some heinous crime, real or believed, past present or future. "What are you doing here, clinic boy?" she asked and Jax said, "Don't call me that," and then, because they had to start somewhere, "Please."

She gave him another suspicious look before she sighed and stuck out her hand. "Tallman. Leta."

"Jax Devreaux."

"What are you looking for out here, Jax Devreaux? And don't tell me you're just looking. I raised three boys and you've got nothing on them."

Jax laughed then, startling himself. "Fossil," he said, and described a piece of bone with his hands. Nothing huge. Just something he could test. "I just need a piece of fossil. Doesn't have to be very big."

He waited. Tallman looked like a woman who enjoyed a puzzle. She squinted at him for a minute. "Now why would you want a piece of fossil, Mr. Devreaux?" she asked. She tapped one fingernail against her front teeth in an unscientific– unhygienic– way and studied him. Just before he broke down and told her her eyes went perfectly big and round as she figured it out. "DNA," she said and started grinning for real. "You've got a sample of DNA. Mr. Devreaux, I am delighted to make your acquaintance."

The sun was directly overhead, so even the trees around the dig site offered no shade. Everything was quiet in the heat. Even the sounds from the neighboring drill site had stopped and most of the other scientists at their site had knocked off until the day cooled down. Jax sat next to Tallman on the edge of the pit, their legs dangling over the side. Jax thought it seemed relaxed but Tallman said the pit was mostly played out. It wasn't a very interesting site. She ate her lunch and offered Jax fruit, junk food and sandwich meat. He accepted water. He'd forgotten his bottle.

"What's an anthropologist doing looking for fossils?" he asked finally. They seemed to be flirting, darting closely around the actual topic. As if neither of them wanted to give anything up too soon. "I thought anthropologists studied people and civilizations. People, not bones." He turned the piece of fossil over and over in his hands as he spoke and Tallman watched the gray/white bone catch sunlight and turn and turn.

"You're here because you think we're doing both, aren't you, Mr. Devreaux?" she asked.

"What do you think?" He wasn't a scientist. He was a social worker who had put two and two together and was wondering if he'd come up with four or six and a half.

Tallman glanced at him and lay back against the dirt, feet on the edge of the pit, hands behind her head. She stared at the sky. "I think it's a new line of theory we've only just begun investigating. I think it knocks a few preconceived notions on their heads." She was quiet for long enough Jax thought she might have fallen asleep. When he turned to look at her Tallman looked back at him right away and said, "I think if it's true someone needs to stop Univers-Oil."

"What makes a place a sacred site?"

She thought about it for a little while. "Usually for most people or civilizations it's a place of power or event. Either something happened at that spot– a battle or the end of a battle, the ending or beginning of a reign or movement. A new idea started there and changed civilization. Or it could be religious/spiritual. The place feels strong. Ley lines or psychic energy." She looked up at the deep sky and the trees around them. "Sometimes it's just beautiful, a place to feel one with nature." From across the plain they could hear Univers-Oil rumbling into action again in the still afternoon.

"Sometimes it's a resting place. Graveyards are sacred." She glanced again at the bone in Jax's hand. "Are you really going to test that, Mr. Devreaux?"

"I don't know," Jax said. "I'm not sure I need to. You seem to think I'd find something-- definite."

Tallman nodded. "Idea's been occurring to quite a few of us. But the Saith aren't big on donating samples of DNA." She stared at him and tapped the fossil. "What do you think you will find, Mr. Devreaux?"

He considered for a minute. It was an alien idea. But it was growing on him. And apparently not only on him. "The truth," Jax said.

He and Mare had a long quiet dinner that night and afterward by mutual unspoken agreement led each other to the bedroom for a long quiet lovemaking. The extra long summer day faded beyond the window and the honeysweet light over Mare's skin made Jax feel lost and lonely, as though she'd already left.

She was going. He knew that even if she didn't yet, as he knew he had to stay. If she left in time, maybe they'd never speak of betrayal. Maybe Jax would never have to ask her how much she knew, how much she had known already when she convinced him to come here.

The honeyed light crept down the wall and after many hours the bedroom was dark and after many hours, Jax slept.

Next day he waited for Ty. She wouldn't be in until afternoon, there was no reason for her to come in early, so he kept his morning appointments, going through the motions in one-on-one counseling, listening to stories of craving and denial, of success and failure– I didn't touch it, I caved in, I'm sorry– and sometimes to the few IP involved in the Rigel equivalent of Earth's heroin, a short session with the sullen bunch whose entire purpose in life appeared to be getting stoned and being immovably unpleasant to everyone around them. Jax had had no patience for them before. He had less now. He canceled his early afternoon appointments and gave Charlynn his easy group in case Ty came early. Daniel stopped at his desk before his own groups.

"Admin is going to bite your head off," he said. He glanced back over his shoulder, making sure Admin was still securely in his office. "What are you doing?" He looked expectant, as if of course Jax would have some good explanation.

"I'm trying to help," Jax said. Wasn't that the official party line?

"You've certainly picked a strange way to go about it," Daniel said.

While he waited, Jax listened to the group going on with Charlynn. They sounded like any Earth group. They made excuses. They refused to answer. The counselor didn't understand. It was a cultural thing. Jax wrote discussion questions on his notepad, questions Charlynn would never ask. Questions that would be considered inappropriate to ask.

*What does an achtonacatl experience feel like?*

*How does it put you in communication, in touch with your Ancestors?*

*Is achtonacatl only found at sacred sites?*

*What is the connection between the sacred sites and Univers-Oil's drill sites?*

*Why can the IP– the Saith– touch the Ancestors better on these sites? What's there?*

He looked at the list and knew he should tear off the page and ball it up and throw it away. He stared at the notepad and thought, *Why are all the fuel sites/drill sites, sacred sites, also sites and places where the Saith can contact their Ancestors in the same places?*

"There you are," Admin said. Jax started. His hands flew forward and he jerked the notepad toward him and couldn't think of anyway to cover so he just stood, holding the pad and facing his boss. "Evaluation time. Thought we could do it today."

Jax didn't say anything. He'd canceled everything before his meeting with Ty, couldn't remember what he had after.

"Looks like you've just got one client this afternoon so that means–"

"I am just starting to make a break through in this case," Jax interrupted and Admin stared at him because no one interrupted Admin. "Look, I know you have to do evals, but not today. Not this case. Not if you want me to be able to–" he swallowed his distaste– "help."

Admin looked at him skeptically, the clinical "*Of course* you've been clean all week, we're just running the bloodwork for our files" look of somebody who has spent many years being lied to. "Everything all right at home?" he asked abruptly and Jax shook his head.

"No. It's not." But that's not it.

Admin smiled, more self satisfied than caring. Of course it was something at home, he'd been in this business a long time, he could tell what was going on with people. "Why don't you schedule some time with a counselor from another clinic? I can give you some names if you–"

"Right. Yes. Good idea." Jax heard the door. Anything

to get Admin to go away. The boss gave him another moment of scrutiny and then said, "Yes. Well. If you want to talk. And I'll get you those contacts."

When Jax turned around Ty was waiting. Sunlight fell through the clinic windows and picked out the scales across her nose and cheeks.

"Let's go for a walk," he said. Unconventional, but borderline acceptable, and suddenly he didn't trust anyone around Ty. He was afraid something would spook her, scare her off before he learned what he needed to know.

They walked a way without speaking, through what was rapidly becoming a town, from the sterile, sterile, cleanwhite clinic they walked into the beauty of Rigel and the store fronts the humans had erected. Almost impressive how quickly Earth forces could bring in ugly, in the form of gas stations and convenience stores and Laundromats— but there was beauty, too. Someone had fashioned their storefront like the Saith's bright and natural habitats, mud and wattle, and flowers planted in the earth that formed the roof and they were busy creating stained glass. The Saith had fallen in love with stained glass instantly. Across from the glaziers was an open air grill where a bored chef from Earth had learned IP cooking and was combining cuisines for humans as well as luring in IP who were curious about the whole notion of having someone else cook for them.

Ty strolled beside him, content and unhurried. Her place in the IP community required nothing more of her for now than that she incubate. And attend meetings to cure her of her dreadful addiction. Jax looked up from his thoughts. Questions fought to go first.

"It's been a week," Ty said before Jax had a chance to say

anything. She glanced at him and looked away, as if trying to decide how she was supposed to behave. "Since I last– used. Oh, I forgot to give you this." She handed him the plastic card, the one he needed to code to reassure everyone concerned that Ty had come to the clinic. He took the card from her and tapped it against the back of his other hand.

"The Saith have been on this planet," he started and stopped, as if that were the whole of the sentence.

"The Saith are of this planet," Ty said.

Jax nodded. "And achtonacatl? How long have the Saith–" he broke off. He didn't want to say "been using." It sounded wrong. "How long as achtonacatl been a part of the culture?" He thought he sounded like a particularly dry history teacher about to direct that question to the sleeping student in the back of the room.

"Our ancestors' ancestors' ancestors found achtonacatl," she said as if the veering conversation didn't phase her. Or as if she could understand where he was headed. "It's the way we contact the Ancestors," she said with subtle emphasis. She moved beside him, relaxed, her hands clasped low behind her back.

"And when it was discovered, what else was going on here? For the Saith?"

"I don't understand," Ty said.

Jax managed not to wave his hand or walk faster. He tried to force his thoughts into order. They refused to go. "When achtonacatl was discovered, when the Saith found it– what else was happening at the same time?"

Ty bobbed her head, the IP equivalent of a shrug. "Everything, of course. As it always is."

"But what– No. All right. Then tell me how it was found." He wanted to shout and yell and run. Even now

Univers-Oil was drilling, digging into the sandy ground of Rigel 5 and changing things forever. Even as they spoke the IP were undergoing counseling and rehabilitation and medical procedures to cure them of their terrible addiction.

"A family was visiting a sacred site, visiting the Ancestors, and the father fell asleep and dreamed. In the dream he collected fungus from the base of the trees for the family meal. He gathered up handfuls of a fungus we'd never eaten before. Tiny little fungi and when the family ate that night the Ancestors came to all of them in their dreams."

"And so they spread the word?"

She slashed her hand diagonally through the air in front of her. *No.* "They went back the next day. They gathered more. And they dreamed again. And when it happened three times they told the rest of the Saith. Not long after our world became cold. For several turns after the stars came from the sky it was cold on Rigel. The Ancestors helped the Saith learn to live through it. Something like that happened for the Ancestors. Something happened to their world– our world– and everything changed and it became cold and there was no one to guide them through it."

And that was what he had been looking for.

She looked at him again, pregnant woman on a hot dusty almost-street, and said, "Do you understand?"

*Too much.* "I do," Jax said and looked up to see they'd circled the so-called block– the long strip of stores and shops and services and possibly hookers he hadn't noticed and that the clinic was up ahead. He changed directions subtly, moving away.

*Why do the sacred sites, Ancestral sites, the places where_'catl is found and the drill sites correspond?*

He swallowed. Ty was watching him. He switched gears.

"When was the first wounded birth?"

She looked surprised. "No one knows that. There have always been wounded births." She put both hands across her stomach.

"But you said there have been more?" Drug counselors believed it was because the drug use of achtonacatl, growing and spreading, use becoming endemic to the IP population.

That wasn't it.

"Since they came," she said, and didn't look at him. "Since the drilling. Things changed. Offspring changed." Her hands pressed against her stomach. He wanted to pull them away and insist everything would be fine.

He couldn't. He didn't know it would be. Oil companies, one after another, fighting each other off, digging and polluting and leaving chemicals behind in the sacred sites where the mushrooms grew.

"Ty, what is the connection the Saith have to the Ancestors?" Just to be certain. Just to be sure.

She looked at him as if he were a total idiot, as if of course he'd figured this out and asked only to tease her. "The Saith are of the Ancestors," she said, and walked away and left him standing alone on the burning street.

Mare's shoes were all lined up in the bedroom door, a line of invisible beings with visible shoes, all pointing forward and ready to go. Mare herself was just out of sight. He could hear her moving around in the bedroom. Jax stopped in the doorway beside the shoes and waited for her to see him. She was stacking clothes on the bed, their jumbled nothing of a closet reduced to two piles, his and hers. She had a box out on the bed beside the piles, but nothing in it. When she turned and her eyes met his, she smiled quick and nervous and said, "I think I'm spring cleaning." A wholly false grin, there and gone.

"No, you're not," Jax said. He didn't move, just watched until the tense moved out of her shoulders and she slid downward to the edge of the bed.

"No, I'm not," she said, and met his gaze again and held it.

"Were you going to tell me?"

Then she looked everywhere but at him. "I think I was. I hope so. Jax, it's not you. It was never you. It's—"

"It's you," he said and she nodded gratefully, as if he understood.

Jax stepped over her shoes and walked into the bedroom. He stared into the empty closet and wondered why she had taken everything out. Was she afraid without visual confirmation he wouldn't believe that she had gone? Wouldn't notice? Was she making a point? Straightening up one last time?

"It was always you, Mare," he said and watched her shoulders begin to go tight again. "The question is, when did you know? Before, during or after? Did you know all along? Is that why you brought me here? Or did you find out once we got here and just decide there was no point in rocking the boat now?" He stood watching and Mare stared at him, her mouth a pretty O of confusion. She raised her hands a little in front of her.

"Jax, what—?"

"Don't. Just don't. You can save face here. Just tell me the truth."

"All right. All right." She rose, stuffed her hands into her back pockets. For all her shoes lined up in the door, Mare was barefoot. "All right. I did know. I did. I mean—

it's an oil company, Jax. Could you really believe their purpose was solely to help people?"

"Isn't that what you kept saying?"

"For *you*. *Your* purpose was to help people." She was starting to get angry. "That's what you do, isn't it? Help people? Even people who don't want your help? I thought you could do it here. I thought we could be together that way."

The anger didn't convince him. His lips thinned, jaw tightened. He wanted to yell, not discuss. "There is a huge difference between trying to help people don't want help and trying to force help on people who don't *need* help," he said. "Univers-Oil set up the clinics as distractions. They sent counselors as pawns. We were supposed to keep the Saith out of their way."

"That doesn't mean you weren't *helping*." She was close to tears. Mare, who often cried when cornered.

"It does when there isn't a problem to help with." He waited, but she didn't interrupt. "Achtonacatl is a harmless hallucinogenic fungus. Earth may not understand or like the belief system that goes with it but so what? Who cares? Earth doesn't have to like or understand it, they just need to leave it alone."

Mare shook her head. Tears looked likely to become angry laughter. "The damn IP and their damn drug. 'Ohh, the Ancestors gave us this drug. Ohh, you're drilling on top of our drugs.'" She glared at him. "I saw you today." Nodded as if he'd argued with her. "With your little alien friend. Your little IP girlfriend. You know after she has her kid she's going to be neuter again? You know that, right?"

"Mare, don't." This wasn't how any of it was supposed to go. Not with the beings he was trying to help. Not with the woman he still loved.

"*Don't*. So rich. 'Mare, don't'. She's not even human, just part of this stupid, stupid planet and the stupid indigenous, intelligent, sentient, *ignorant* life forms on it. You know that, don't you?" She as starting to spit as she talked, her entire body so tense he thought she'd shatter. "She's just another one of the people you *can't help*. And I knew. I knew they were just using you. Clinics. Counselors. Foils."

"You knew." His voice sounded ragged but calm. He wasn't certain what he was going to say.

"I did. I knew. I knew so long ago–"

"When did you realize the IP were related to the Ancestors?"

She barely stumbled, caught herself instantly. "Of course they are. Ancestors. They're always babbling about their ancestors. Ancestors means dead, doesn't it?" She started packing again, haphazardly; things went into the box with no thought.

Jax gave her a minute and then, quietly, asked, "When did you realize the Ancestors are the fossils, the fuel that Univers-Oil is drilling? When did you realize the drill sites are ancestral sites are sacred sites where the means to contact them grows?"

Mare went still. Her eyes were fixed on his face, unmoving. She rocked a little with the force of her heartbeat. The hand that held one of his shoes and a book that had vanished under something a month ago shook just a little. When she finally spoke again she said very quietly, "What did you say?"

She sounded afraid.

Dawn found them together on the bedroom floor, backs

against the bed, fingers interlaced. Water bottles lay around them, empty and discarded. They hadn't spoken for over an hour, just sat together watching an alien dawn spread across skies that weren't theirs. Hunger finally forced them up, into the kitchenette.

"For what it's worth," Mare said, peering hopefully into the cold box which was hopelessly empty, "I wouldn't have missed it for the world."

"Yes, you would have," Jax said. He tapped her on the shoulder and offered her fruit he'd found on the counter. The house was mostly empty. He needed to shop.

"Yes, I would have." She turned back to her explorations and made a triumphant sound, then backed out of the cold box. "There's something alive in there."

"New scientific find?"

"Really old bread." She discarded it. "I'll take the report to Univers-Oil," she said. She'd given up hunting food and started eating the apple he'd given her.

"All right." She might. She might not. Word would obviously be going out instantly. Leta and the scientists were going forward. Jax would go to the social workers at the clinics. He mostly thought Mare needed to spread the word for her own sake. He wasn't sure she realized that.

"For what it's worth, Mare, I'm going to miss you."

"No, you're not," she said, and gave him a small smile before she left to pack her shoes.

"Yes, I am," Jax said quietly.

They met up with the crazy flyboy midday. Mare took one look at Ryc and gave Jax a look that clearly accused him of trying to have her killed. Jax laughed and kissed her, and kissed her again for good measure, handed her off to Ryc, waved, and walked away before the scooter even left the jump point.

He headed directly to the clinic. There was work that needed doing. He needed to talk to other people who were there to help.

Clinic, day 61. Midday and no one in when he got there. Jax dropped to his desk and sat staring at the files there, half inclined to box them up, more inclined to let them lay. Silliness. Folly. He should have seen it. They all should have.

He heard the door open and felt the rush of light and heat. When he looked up, he realized he'd been waiting for her to walk in all day.

Jennifer Rachel Baumer lives, writes, runs and procrastinates in the Northern Nevada desert where she lives with her husband and cats in the rural North Valleys, surrounded by jackrabbits, cottontails, coyotes and quail... and possibly ghosts.

Her work can be found in genre magazines and anthologies, both virtual and print, and in the previous collection The Last Oracle & Other Ghostly Tales, available through Amazon.
She also maintains a rather hit or miss blog at
http://jenniferrbaumer.blogspot.com/

A lonely woman in a surreal city haunts her own life.
A new house in a new neighborhood reveals its ghastly secrets.
And the grimoire discovered in the local used bookstore proves to
be more than just a curiosity.

How clear is the line between life and death – or between the living
and the dead? What happens at the Renaissance Faire when death
in the form of the Danse Macabre doesn't pass by?

In this collection of nine haunting tales, award-winning author
Jennifer Rachel Baumer reveals the secrets of the dead, and the
ghosts of the living.

Two young seekers looking for knowledge in the City of Answers come perilously close to dying for truth.

A woman fighting to remain sane in the face of insanity finds the cure is worse than the disease and the end doesn't always justify the means.

In two stories of sacrifice, one woman learns just how hard change is and that progress comes at a price, and a young couple have to decide if the good of the many truly outweighs the good of the few – or the family.

And in the title story, a group of friends learn just what's behind the locked door that offers questionable refuge from the rain.

In this collection of six urban horror stories, award-winning author Jennifer Rachel Baumer looks at the horror found within cities – and within the people inside them.

Ghosts of the Dead  Ghosts of the Living

A woman on the run from an abusive marriage stumbles over gravestones for the living and renews her journey to reclaiming her lost life.

A serial killer prowls the night-dark highways, collecting souls of the living and the dead.

A misjudgment in cultural etiquette nearly spells doom for a young bride at the hands of her angry mother-in-law.

A portal between life and death disguised as a bathroom mirror leads an unhappy wife on a new journey.

A family history that foretells the future is practically writing itself. A drifter on the run from events he can't quite remember takes questionable refuge with a modern-day Dorian Gray.

In this collection of six ghostly tales, award-winning author Jennifer Rachel Baumer takes a journey into unnamed and unknown cities and the surreal darkness within them.